Nick watched A
and shook his h

For twelve months he'...
that she was a spoilt, selfish, self-indulgent social-
ite. She was funny—yes! Intriguing? Definitely!
Seductive? Don't think about it! And fascinating
beyond words! But she lacked compassion, he'd
reminded himself, had no understanding of other
people's lives and problems. And she was without
commitment to anything, without ambition or a
sense of duty—the things that were so important
to him!

Having pursued many careers—from school-teaching to pig farming—with varying degrees of success and plenty of enjoyment, **Meredith Webber** seized on the arrival of a computer in her house as an excuse to turn to what had always been a secret urge—writing. As she had more doctors and nurses in the family than any other professional people, the medical romance seemed the way to go! Meredith lives on the Gold Coast of Queensland, with her husband and teenage son.

Recent titles by the same author:

WINGS OF DUTY
COURTING DR GROVES
PRACTICE IN THE CLOUDS
FLIGHT INTO LOVE

WINGS OF PASSION

BY
MEREDITH WEBBER

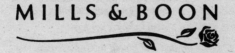

MILLS & BOON

*First published in Great Britain 1996
Harlequin Mills & Boon Limited,
Eton House, 18-24 Paradise Road, Richmond, Surrey TW9 1SR*

© Meredith Webber 1996

ISBN 0 263 80017 2

*Set in Times 10 on 11½ pt. by
Rowland Phototypesetting Limited
Bury St Edmunds, Suffolk*

03-9702-47623-D

*Printed and bound in Great Britain
by Mackays of Chatham PLC, Chatham*

CHAPTER ONE

THE island appeared as a dark hump in the lighter darkness of the sea. Even with the low cloud-cover obscuring all light from the moon and stars, Allysha could define a different texture in the shadowy land mass. She eased the plane into a turn, watching for the lights of the resort she knew should be nestling in the sheltered southern bay.

'Sure you've got the right island?'

Peter's voice reminded her she had a passenger.

'It had better be!' she told him. 'Flying across water under low cloud is not my favourite occupation and, if this isn't it, I wouldn't know where to look next.'

The lights of the resort appeared as she replied and she sighed deeply. Her instruments had told her it was here, but Peter's teasing question had raised a too-ready doubt.

'They've lit their strip,' Peter pointed out, and she peered ahead to see the island's small runway neatly marked by two rows of headlights.

'Headlights?' she muttered, banking the plane as she swung around to line up with the marked space.

'They must be golf buggies,' Peter said, as they dropped lower. 'There are at least twenty of them and I know the island resort boasts one truck and a small forklift. I suppose it would be sure to have buggies to save wealthy legs the strain of walking.'

He sounded slightly envious, as if the life of the rich and famous who frequented this exclusive resort was a tantalising dream—for ever beyond his reach.

'I'm going to circle again,' Allysha told him, forgetting everything else as she concentrated on holding the plane steady in the cross-winds that buffeted its fragile shell. 'If the wind catches us at the wrong moment, we'll slew sideways and probably wipe out half their fleet.'

She brought the plane around again, fighting the drag of the flaps and dropping lower and lower, until she was only metres above the ground when she lined up the lights.

'There must have been easier ways of proving myself!'

She felt the wheels touch down and pulled the throttle back to zero thrust, battling to hold the aircraft steady in the avenue of light.

'Proving yourself! So that's at the heart of the mystery!'

She was conscious of Peter speaking, but ignored his words while she concentrated on their safety.

'The wind's getting worse,' she said, turning to him when she was certain that she was in control of everything. 'Can we grab your patient and be off as quickly as possible?'

He was looking at her in an assessing kind of way and she frowned at him, puzzled by his expression. Peter had asked her out when she'd first arrived at Rainbow Bay and she'd made it clear to him that she wasn't interested in him, or men in general—not even in the most casual of relationships.

'Proving yourself to whom?' he asked, as she halted the plane outside the tiny shed that was the island's air terminal.

'What are you dithering on about?' she demanded.

Her earlier grumble, which had eased aloud from her subconscious, was forgotten now that they were safely on the ground. 'Let's get this heart attack chap on board and get going.'

She urged him towards the rear of the plane, passing him to open the door while he unstrapped his equipment bags.

'What will I carry?'

After six months as a pilot for the Royal Flying Doctor Service she was used to helping out on evacuation flights. Straightforward evacuations were often accomplished with only the pilot and a nurse on board the plane, with the pilot acting as stretcher bearer or general assistant. For this flight, according to Peter who'd taken the call from the resident nurse at the resort, there'd been a specific request for a doctor.

'And as the resort nurse sounded hysterical and quite unable to cope,' Peter had said when he'd repeated the conversation, 'I thought I'd better come with you.'

She followed him into the cabin and picked up the small bag he indicated.

'Defibrillator, just in case,' he said, leading the way down the steps and across to a dark huddle of people outside the terminal building. He had a bulky bag slung over his shoulder and a stretcher tucked under his arm—enough equipment to stabilise a life! The wonder of what they did crept over her again, warming some of the cold and empty places in her heart, then she remembered she was his helper and hurried after him.

Catching up when he paused to speak to someone, she stayed behind him, holding the case, as they were ushered inside the small hut.

Peter bent over his patient and she stepped closer.

'Allysha Craig! Well, well, well!'

She started and looked around, then realised that Peter's movement must have revealed her to the man on the makeshift bed.

'We all wondered where you'd got to when you left our happy circle so precipitously,' Brent James said, while his glance slid over her neat uniform. He must have registered her connection with the doctor who was taking his blood pressure for he added, 'Not pretending we're a nurse, are we, darling?'

The malicious glee in his voice made the hairs on her arms prickle, but she bit back the angry denial that sprang to her lips.

'Where's the pain?'

Peter's voice was curt enough to startle Allysha and she pushed back the encroaching memories, ignored the sick feeling in the pit of her stomach and concentrated on Peter's actions. He might need her to hold an infusion bag or pass him equipment or drugs, and she had to be alert to his commands.

Brent began explaining about his previous heart attacks, and Allysha risked a quick glance at him. Still overweight, he had a shiny redness about his face that, to her, suggested he'd lost none of his fondness for overindulgence in good food and fine wine.

'. . .and the Anginine had no effect. I contacted the nurse immediately, of course.'

Allysha glanced beyond him at the blonde in a vivid pink uniform, who was batting her eyelashes hopefully in Peter's direction.

No joy for you there once you'd shown unprofessional panic on the phone, she thought, then recognised the edge of cynicism that Nick had hated in her.

She glared at Brent James, who had prodded uncomfortable and unwanted recollections back to life so that they could press on the bruised places in her heart. He must have finished listing his symptoms for he turned towards her, probably in time to catch the animosity in her eyes.

'Well, little Allysha, you've found yourself a new doctor to provide diversions?' he queried silkily, then he gasped as Peter pressed a needle through his skin.

Allysha bit her lip and turned away from the mockery in Brent's over-bright eyes.

'You seem to know this chap,' Peter muttered to her, bending over his bag to hide the movement of his lips. 'Could he be putting on an act? I don't think there's anything wrong with him.'

'Perhaps you could defibrillate him anyway!' Allysha suggested bitterly.

Peter straightened slightly and his eyes met hers, a thousand questions lurking in their blueness.

'Could he be on drugs?'

The only question she hadn't expected! She looked at Brent—over-excited, restless, definitely stimulated! She thought for a moment, trying to remember if anyone in the group had ever offered her drugs, then shrugged.

'Coke, maybe,' she said, reluctance and doubt dragging at the words. Brent belonged to a fast crowd always on the lookout for new thrills, and the knowledge that she had once been part of it shamed her.

Peter frowned and bent over the bag again—really searching for something this time. As he straightened she saw another questioning glance directed her way and then he was giving orders, arranging for Brent to be lifted onto the stretcher by hovering staff members and transported to the plane.

Allysha picked up the equipment case she'd carried

from the plane, and followed the little procession. Peter remained behind, talking to the nurse. She hurried on, knowing that she would have to show the men how to slide the stretcher into position on the aircraft and then fasten it for the return journey.

'Going to hold my hand on the journey back to the mainland, Nursie?' Brent asked as she bent over him to check that the stretcher was secure. 'I'll be flying straight home from Rainbow Bay so I won't have a chance to talk to you later.'

Sly, knowing pleasure sparkled in his eyes and she turned away from the silent suggestion of complicity, shivering at the uneasiness it caused. Ignoring his question, she walked up front and sank into her seat, checking her flight plan and beginning pre-flight procedures with determined concentration.

'All set!'

Peter's voice was her cue to check the door. She knew he would have locked it, but it was a habit she couldn't break. She brushed past their patient, slid her hand over the lock to confirm its position and then returned to her seat. Once there she let the familiar preparatory sounds and motions soothe away her agitation.

Flying had always excited her and she'd worked hard to perfect her skill. She knew her expertise was respected by her peers, and Eddie Stone, the Base's chief pilot, had commended her ability. It was he who had entrusted her with tonight's tricky, low-level flight.

'Staying low?'

She nodded in reply to Peter's question as he slid into the co-pilot's seat.

'It's a short hop, and the cloud mass is so deep we'd barely be up above it before we'd have to come down again,' she explained, then raised her eyebrows as Peter slipped on a pair of headphones and waved his hand towards the set that hung over the back of her seat.

She put them on without argument, realising that he must want to say something to her without their passenger hearing it.

'I told that fellow we'd radio base for an ambulance to meet the plane and transfer him to hospital, and he said he didn't need one.'

Peter sounded puzzled, and more than a little annoyed.

'I told you you should have defibrillated him,' Allysha replied, fury that Brent James might be using them for a free ride boiling through her blood. 'I'll bet he's got his swanky Lear parked at Rainbow Bay. I presume he'll fly straight home to his specialist in Sydney.'

'Lear?'

Peter sounded so puzzled that she had to smile.

'Jet plane! As in big boys' toys!' Sarcasm sparked the words from her tongue. 'His pilot has probably been sleeping in a tent on the edge of the airfield while Brent was pampering himself in a thousand-dollar-a-night luxury suite at the island.'

'Did you fly for him once?' Peter asked, obviously intrigued by her knowledge of their patient and probing for clues to her past.

Allysha had kept herself aloof from the other staff members at the Base, at first because she'd been too heartsick to care about socialising. The strain of pretending to an interest she no longer felt in anything would have been too much for her as she took those first tentative steps towards a new life. Then solitude became a habit, and she had found it hard to break out of the isolation she had coiled, like a snail's protective shell, around herself.

'I knew him once.' She hoped both words and tone would prevent further questions, but she had underestimated Peter's interest.

'When you knew another doctor who provided you with "diversions"?'

Her stomach cramped violently and she had to cling to the controls for support. She felt sweat break out on her forehead and knew her hair would stick spikily to it, revealing her agitation.

'Brent James belonged to a group of people I knew a long time ago,' she said carefully. 'That's it, Peter.'

She looked across at him, aware that her eyes would be pleading for him to understand that she didn't want to talk about the past—or think about it!

The winds which had made landing and take-off difficult were behind them now and the lights of the airport, built out over land reclaimed from one corner of the Bay, were winking their welcome.

'Are you going to insist he goes to hospital?' she asked, trying to get the conversation—or her thoughts—back onto practical matters.

'I can't,' Peter admitted. 'But I'd damned well like to send him a bill for transport.'

'The Royal Flying Doctor Service is free to all members of the public,' Allysha quoted, then radioed their approach to the control tower.

'But the Government can charge for air and sea rescue searches if they feel the people involved have acted irresponsibly,' Peter pointed out. 'Maybe we could set a precedent, arguing irresponsibility! Or perhaps he might give us a donation or leave us the Lear in his will!'

'You wish!' Allysha told him, bringing the plane in

to land with less than her usual flair. She throttled back the engines with unnecessary sharpness. 'He wouldn't give a starving man his crusts!'

Aware of Peter's interest, she breathed deeply—trying to conquer the turmoil in her mind and body. It didn't matter that Brent James had seen her—that he knew where she was! He didn't matter any more than the rest of those so-called friends of the past had mattered.

Yet, even as she reassured herself, the unease she was trying to banish shifted within her, stirring more trepidation to life.

Peter unbuckled his seat belt and returned to his patient, while Allysha brought the plane to a halt outside the RFDS hangar. She unclenched her fingers. Of course those people didn't matter! her mind cried in silent denial. But the shock of seeing Brent had jolted her, letting the pain of the past sneak through her defences and settle in her heart again.

'My pilot should be waiting.'

As Allysha cut the engines and walked back to open the door she heard Brent's words, and wondered if Peter felt as much like hitting the man as she did.

'I'd like you to sign this before you go,' Peter said in a steely voice that answered Allysha's unspoken thought. She turned to watch what was happening between the two men.

'Sign something?' Brent blustered, immediately suspicious.

'It's a statement that you have taken yourself out of our hands,' Peter explained, passing over a small notebook. 'A minor incident like the one you've suffered is often a precursor to a much more serious infarct. I wouldn't like your family to imply we were in any way negligent if you have a fatal attack on your trip home.'

Allysha tightened her lips to stop them smiling, while Brent's cheeks lost their rosy hue and his face became drained and grey-looking.

'It could have been an ordinary angina attack I had earlier,' he protested. 'I've had them before.'

'But you said the Anginine didn't relieve the pain,' Peter pointed out, waving the notebook insistently in front of his confused patient. 'Hard to tell the difference sometimes. Please sign.'

Brent tried to sit up but the straps holding him to the stretcher were still in place and all he could do was look around, as if distracted by his loss of control over the situation.

'Perhaps I should go to hospital,' he muttered. 'Have tests and things. You've a private hospital in this town? You could get me in?'

'The public hospital has some private beds, but you'd have to be processed through Accident and Emergency first,' Peter told him, and again Allysha had to hide a smile at their patient's reaction. She doubted Brent had ever been in a public anything—and as for being 'processed'!

She slipped past them back into her seat to complete the shut-down procedures.

'Mr James with you people?'

She saw Peter look towards the open door.

'Are you his pilot?'

She heard a mumbled affirmation. Brent must have been supremely confident of his acting ability to have phoned his pilot before he left the resort.

'Well, what's it to be?' Peter asked in an implacable voice. 'Your signature and a quick trip home, or shall we call up the ambulance and send you off to the cheerful ministrations of Rainbow Bay Public Hospital?'

She almost saw the answering shudder pass through the man's frame, and knew that he was regretting his rash behaviour. But the Brent Jameses of this world were never down for long, she reminded herself.

'You're a doctor,' Brent said, a strengthening in his voice confirming her opinion of his character, 'and you've got all the gear you need. Why don't I pay you to fly down to Sydney with me, then get my pilot to fly you back up tomorrow?'

Brent beamed up at Peter, totally unaware of the other man's mounting fury.

'Because I'm an ethical, principled man, Mr James!' Peter ground out. 'Words that obviously have no meaning for you. Sometime tonight a person may genuinely need my services and I will be here waiting for that call, not indulging the whim of an idle layabout who thinks money can buy anything. Now, will you please sign this release so we can let you out of here. I've a feeling Allysha wants to fumigate the plane.'

Allysha watched Brent James sign, but the controlled fury in his fingers as he dug the pen into the flimsy paper worsened her internal turmoil. He was a vindictive man. . .

'Right!' Peter spoke briskly. 'Straps undone; you're free to go.'

He didn't reach out to help the older man sit up, and the pilot, hovering in the darkness beyond the door, was obviously uneasy about his role and unwilling to clamber up into the RFDS plane. Their patient struggled to a sitting position, muttering obscenities Allysha was glad she couldn't hear, then he turned towards her with a look of such malevolent malice that she shrank back against the seat and huddled her arms protectively around her body.

'I'll repeat my judgement that you should go to the hospital,' Peter said, reaching out his hand to steady his patient down the steps to level ground. He turned to the pilot.

'You can be a witness to that,' he added, prompting a further burst of invective from Brent.

'He's my pilot and he only hears what I say to him,' he roared, so irate that Allysha wondered if he might have a genuine heart attack right there on the tarmac.

Peter shrugged.

'OK!' he said easily, then he climbed back into the cabin.

Allysha was stripping the cover from the stretcher and trying to pretend that she wasn't shaking all over.

'I'll drive you home,' Peter said.

'Don't be ridiculous,' she told him. 'That flight was two hours' flying time. I'm still on call and will need my car to get back here if there's another emergency.'

'I'm also on call,' he pointed out, bending to help her lock the collapsible stretcher into its storage space. 'So, if we're called out, I'll collect you on my way to the airport. If not, I'll drive you down to collect your car whenever you like in the morning.'

Allysha straightened up and looked at Peter. Was it because he was good-looking that she'd been immediately suspicious of him? And why was he being nice to her? He had a reputation as a womaniser. Was he doing some groundwork for another invitation out?

Her gaze scanned his face, but the blue eyes showed only kindness.

'It's OK to need help occasionally,' he said, then he reached out and drew her against his chest. She rested there for a moment, aware of how long it had been since she'd had any physical contact with another human being. 'You can't go on coping alone—proving yourself—without any social interaction or friendships or relaxation. It's not natural or healthy!'

He rubbed his hand across her head, ruffling her short brown hair, then reached down to tilt her chin so that she had to look up at him.

'I'm speaking as a doctor, Allysha of the beautiful brown eyes!' he said very seriously. 'And as someone who would like to be your friend.'

Did he see a flicker of doubt in her face?

'Friend!' he repeated with extra emphasis, then his face relaxed and his daredevil grin reappeared. 'For lovers I prefer blondes. Even someone as cut off from the gossip as you must have heard that on the grapevine by now!'

She saw the smile but wondered how deep the jocularity went. Peter was showing her an unexpected sympathy and she knew, if they were to become friends, she would be forced to look beyond the carefree playboy image he projected.

She pushed herself away from him.

'I will drive myself home,' she told him. 'I'm OK now.' She looked up into his eyes and smiled. 'But thanks for the offer,' she added. 'It meant a lot to me.'

'The offer of a lift might have been refused,' he said quietly, 'but the offer of friendship stands.'

He held out his hand and, surprised but warmed by the gesture, she took it and shook it in a silent pledge to the possibilities ahead.

He squeezed her fingers gently then released them, bending to retrieve his bag of drugs.

'Well, let's get this lot locked away, and head for

home,' he said cheerfully. 'Want to take a small bet we're called out again before the night's out?'

'Eddie Stone has ''Don't bet with Peter'' printed like a letterhead across the top of his memo forms,' Allysha replied, smiling at her new-found friend.

'Well, I like that!' Peter grumbled, leading the way across the tarmac. 'He bets with me all the time—and wins more often than he loses! Probably makes more money out of me than he does as chief pilot.'

As Allysha felt her smile broadening she knew an ease she hadn't felt for a long time. Peter had opened a tiny chink in her defensive armour, and the icy tension of self-protection was beginning to thaw.

'Did Jack tell you he's got a doctor lined up to take Matt's place?' Peter asked, unlocking the side door that gave access to the hangar and snapping on the interior lights.

'Eddie mentioned it.' Allysha crossed to the sturdy cabinets and waited while Peter unlocked them. 'I hope he's committed enough to see out a full year. The people on my clinic runs have had more doctors than diseases lately.'

'Matt's leaving was certainly a shock,' Peter agreed, bending over his bag to retrieve the drugs that would have to go into the cold storage. 'But it was one of those unavoidable things—with his father dying like that.'

He handed Allysha a tray of drugs and fluids to hold, then pushed the bag into place and locked the door.

'According to Jack,' he continued, 'this fellow's willing to give us a year, and he should be good. He's been in the United States working with an emergency medical flight team. Seems over there they do a lot of flight medicine, ferrying people from small hospitals to specialist facilities that might be two or three hours' flying time away.'

Allysha was surprised.

'And I thought we were unique!' she said, carrying the tray to the cold storage cabinet and waiting while Peter unlocked it. This procedure always caused delays, both in taking off and in finalising flights, but drug security and correct storage were of paramount importance.

'We are rare in that we have regular patients separated by thousands of miles and in the services our clinic flights provide, but our emergency and evacuation work is being replicated all over the world. First-response teams, who pride themselves on getting to an accident within half an hour and providing pro-active medical treatment on the spot, are being set up in most countries, and air transport is being used more and more.'

Allysha smiled. Peter's 'lover-boy' image disappeared when he was talking about work. He might play hard when he was off duty, but no one who had ever worked with him could doubt his commitment to the Service.

'You love it, don't you?' she said gently as he slid his arm around her shoulders and steered her across the hangar floor. He reached up to pull the chains that would open the big doors while she started the little machine that would tow the aircraft back to the hangar.

'I do!' he admitted, walking beside her and smiling down into her face. 'To me it's a constant challenge. I know, theoretically, we do more humdrum clinic work than emergency stuff, but every time I'm called to an evac flight I feel the surge of excitement that I foolishly imagined being a doctor was all about.'

He looked slightly embarrassed about this

confession, but Allysha was intrigued enough to probe a little further.

'The excitement of the flight—of getting to your patient no matter where he is—or the excitement of the challenge you might find when you arrive?' She hooked the steel cable of the dolly through the nose loop on the plane.

He looked at her for a moment and then he said, so quietly his tone provided a strange emphasis, 'I know it sounds stupid, but my excitement is that of a fighter— and it's me against death!'

He laughed, as if the words were the product of midnight fantasies and should not be taken seriously, but Allysha knew that she was hearing something he had probably never told anyone before. She started the engine on the towing dolly, letting Peter talk as she steered the big aircraft towards its position in the huge, curved shed that housed the three RFDS planes.

'As a kid I used to read about gladiators—but I knew no one fought exhibition matches against lions any more,' he said. 'In fact, if you discount the Mafia and mercenaries in African countries with unpronounceable names, no one fights anyone or anything much these days. Yet I was always looking for that ultimate challenge! I was certain it must exist for me—somewhere.'

He paused for so long that Allysha thought the confessions were finished. She stopped the machine, unhooked it and pushed it to the side of the hangar. Peter hadn't followed her inside, and she turned to see his shadow in the doorway. Something in the stillness of the man held her silent.

She waited, watching him slump back against the doorframe and tip his head up as if to study the underside of the clouds.

'My mother died when I was sixteen, and I found my enemy,' he said quietly. 'Death became the enemy I could pit my skills against!'

Oh, hell! she thought, feeling the emotion churning up inside her but unable to find any words that might convey what she was feeling.

'Pure soap-box stuff, I suppose,' he added in a slightly lighter but still strained voice. 'Not something I talk about much at all!'

He grinned as she joined him in the doorway and she knew he was recovering.

'Don't look so upset,' he urged her, reaching out to clasp her shoulders and shaking her gently. 'It was a long time ago and it led me into a life I love, but it's been a night of revelations—one way or another.'

She smiled at him.

'I'm glad you told me that,' she said, feeling as if she'd been given a special gift, an extra pledge of the friendship that might develop between them. 'But don't think it will lead to any reciprocal arrangements!' she warned him. 'My past is a tacky, uninspiring story that bears so little resemblance to reality it's not worth repeating. Seeing Brent James was a shock—but shocks are used as therapy, remember, and maybe it's done me some good.'

He leaned forward and dropped a kiss on the top of her head.

'Prove it by coming to the welcome barbecue for the new doctor on Saturday night,' he challenged. 'In fact, come with me. My current blonde has gone south to visit her parents, and it will give the staff something to talk about. We've been sadly lacking in enlivening gossip since Matt whisked our sweet Lucia out from under our noses!'

'But I never go to staff functions,' she objected, reaching out for the chains that would lower the doors.

'Never went to them!' he corrected. 'All that is about to change. We can give them all a double whammy! Not only will they have Allysha Craig turning up at a function but she'll be turning up attached securely to my arm.'

Allysha chuckled, and they switched off the lights and made their way out of the dark hangar through the small door.

'It would certainly cause waves!' she agreed, then added, 'But we go as friends, Peter, nothing more!'

He nodded, wiping away his smile and holding one hand to his heart.

'Nothing more!' he promised, then grinned again and added, 'I told you—I'm a blonde man!'

Airport security drove up, and Allysha waved to the man in the small vehicle to show they were ready to leave.

Peter turned towards her and said, 'There's usually a right time for change in our lives, Allysha. Maybe your meeting up with that fellow was a kind of signal from the fates that you have to get on with yours.'

Allysha nodded. Maybe Peter was right.

Maybe Peter was right?

She looked up at him.

'You're ruining your image, you know,' she scolded. 'First kindness, and now philosophy! From Peter the Playboy? Who would have believed it?'

He tried to look affronted and only succeeded in looking so ridiculous that she had to laugh.

'Now, don't go telling anyone!' he warned.

'About Saturday? Or your kindness?' she teased.

'Neither!' he said severely. 'I've worked hard on my

image. I don't want it all blown to bits by some idle chat from you! And as for Saturday—you don't want to spoil the effect. Can't you imagine Susan's face?'

Allysha chuckled, warmed by the camaraderie that had been missing from her life for too long.

'Susan has a heart of solid gold beneath her matron's manner,' she said, defending her boss's wife automatically. 'She just likes to know what's going on with all the people she sees as "her charges".'

'You're right,' Peter agreed. 'She's actually one of my favourite people, and that's no reason to spoil a surprise.'

He touched her lightly on the top of her head and added, 'The party's at six. I'll collect you at five to,' before walking across to his car.

CHAPTER TWO

'Wow!'

Peter's exclamation made Allysha smile, but inside it helped prop up her wavering courage.

'As well as blondes I do like long hair, but if anyone could sway me into changing my allegiances it could be a dark-eyed beauty with a shiny cap of sun-flecked brown hair and lips that men can dream about.'

Ignoring the amused glances from people in the lobby of her apartment block, he turned her around and she allowed the inspection, knowing the coral-coloured cotton dress suited her lightly tanned skin and shapely but petite figure.

'Susan will never believe it!' he announced at last, a satisfied smile quirking his lips upward at the corners. 'And if this new fellow isn't already attached, you'll make him wonder why he didn't come to Rainbow Bay years ago!'

'OK!' Allysha told him, noticing how handsome he was in casual shorts and a dark blue shirt which accentuated the colour of his eyes. 'That's enough flattery for a month! Let's get this over and done with.'

Peter pretended to look shocked.

'You're going out to enjoy yourself,' he protested, 'not heading to the dentist for root canal work.'

Allysha smiled again.

'And I think I might enjoy myself,' she promised, and walked with him out to the little red sports car that was his first love.

24

The welcome party was being held in the back yard at Eddie and Susan Stone's house—an ideal location as it boasted a cool blue pool with a fern-shaded barbecue area beyond it and sufficient paving for chairs and tables to be set casually around.

As Peter and Allysha approached they heard splashing and shrieks of laughter from the pool.

'Sounds like the Stone twins trying to drown Leonie's kids,' Peter said. 'Do you know the terrible teenagers?'

Allysha nodded.

'I met the twins when I flew them home from "Wetherby" in Eddie's little Cessna last school holidays. He was stranded out at Cameron River after a bird strike damaged the engine and I dropped the mechanic and spare parts out there, then collected Lachlan and Stewart for him.'

'And you didn't consider it would be a favour to mankind in general to suggest they try parachuting out over some remote spot?' Peter teased, and Allysha chuckled.

They had reached the gate that led into the back yard and stood for a moment, leaning over it, while they watched the four teenagers frolicking in the pool.

'I like the twins,' she admitted, then looked directly into Peter's eyes before she added, 'I was considered a lost cause at the same age—wild and wilful! Perhaps it's fellow-feeling.'

He raised his eyebrows and studied her intently for a moment before he smiled.

'The cool, controlled, quiet Allysha? Well, well! Getting to know you *is* proving interesting,' he said. 'Now, shall we plunge into the heart of these festivities and give Susan the surprise of her life?'

They pushed through the gate and rounded the corner of the house, walking warily along the side of the swimming pool to avoid the arching plumes of water being flung up by the swimmers' exuberance.

'Look at Susan's face!' Peter muttered, tucking Allysha's arm more securely through the crook of his elbow.

Allysha had a glimpse of Susan's open-mouthed surprise, then her fingers tightened into claws and bit into Peter's arm as she tried to stay upright. Her knees shook, her heart stopped beating, her breathing went haywire and her stomach turned cartwheels.

Peter, sensing her distress—or maybe in agony from her convulsive grip—stopped and turned towards her.

'Blondes! You only like blondes?' she demanded, knowing the desperation in her voice would be reflected in her eyes.

'Definitely!' he confirmed, a frown of concern appearing between his eyebrows.

'Good,' she said and straightened up, squaring her shoulders and quelling her internal agitation. 'Then we'll neither of us be hurt by a little bit of play-acting.'

Peter looked as stunned as she had felt a few seconds earlier, but there was no time for explanations. With a grim determination she stretched up on tip toes and kissed him on the lips.

'You're my latest lover,' she murmured, 'so act a little lover-like!'

She pushed his unresisting body in the direction of the gathering, aware that all the adults in the group were now watching their approach. Leonie Cooper, the base manager, was there, and Eddie Stone, the chief pilot; Bill, one of the other pilots, with his wife and young baby; Katie, the radio officer, with an unhappy droop to the corners of her mouth; Jack Gregory, the senior doctor, and more. A mass of familiar faces, yet amongst them all she saw only one.

It was a dark, intense looking face with a firm but beautifully shaped mouth and a fine, no-nonsense nose. Wavy black hair that would flop, when it needed cutting, onto a high forehead and deep-set brown eyes that could melt with love or flash with angry yellow fire but were now, she guessed, as hard as river-washed pebbles.

'Lovely to see you, Allysha!'

Susan had surged forward out of the still life of staff members, and was now positively gabbling her greetings.

'We didn't realise—or know—Peter didn't—or—'

'I persuaded her it was time to be more social,' Peter said, rescuing his hostess from her tangled half-sentences. 'After all, social is my middle name.'

Susan looked from one to the other, a thousand questions in her eyes, then she shrugged and turned towards the house.

'Go and introduce yourselves to the new fellow,' she suggested. 'I've got salads to carry out.'

'We'll help,' Allysha suggested immediately, and tried to drag Peter after their hostess.

'Later!' he said. 'First we meet the new doctor.' He spoke deliberately and she knew he had guessed the source of her sudden agitation.

'After all,' he whispered when Susan was out of earshot, 'you'll have to face him some time. You can only take so long to carry salads out of the house!'

He slid his hand over Allysha's, and as he prised open her fingers he whispered, 'I can take the hint

and I won't leave your side, but you're cutting off the
circulation in my thumb.'

She fixed a smile in place, and let him hold the hand
which had been clinging tightly to his arm.

'Ready?' he asked, his voice gruff with what could
have been concern.

'No!' she whispered, but she moved with him, stepping courageously towards the man she had thought
she would never see again.

'Peter and Allysha!'

Jack Gregory, at the far end of the covered area,
called to them and beckoned. 'Come and meet Nick
Furlong.'

Allysha saw Peter's glance flick from Nick to her,
and could almost hear the gears clicking over in
his mind.

'I'm glad you came, Allysha,' Jack continued as they
drew closer. 'Nick will probably be taking over Matt's
rosters so it will give you a chance to get to know him
before you fly him and Christa on the two-day clinic
flight next week.'

Peter's hand was getting slippery and she wondered
which of them was sweating. She clung on, unwilling
to release this clammy hold on reality.

'Nick and I met when he was at Broken Hill,' she
said carefully, drawing closer and closer to Peter's side.
She raised her head and flashed a quick look in Nick's
direction, deliberately keeping her eyes unfocused so
she couldn't see him clearly.

Jack looked surprised, but he recovered quickly.

'Oh, well, that's good,' he said, then continued with
his introductions. 'Nick Furlong, meet Peter Flint.' He
ushered Nick forward towards the newcomers.

Allysha decided that she couldn't look at him again;

couldn't bear to see whatever emotion might be lurking in his eyes. She bent her head, studying her feet, and Peter's feet, and Jack's—surprisingly clad in clean white and purple joggers—and then the dusty riding boots she'd bought for Nick one day—a long time ago—telling him that black lace-ups were for city folk!

'Did you work for the RFDS in Broken Hill?' Peter asked. She heard Nick's assent and, in the peripheral vision allowed by her downward concentration, she saw Peter's hand appear, to be clasped by another hand—finely boned, the fingers long and lean yet full of strength.

Her mind whirled into chaos as she remembered the feeling of those fingers on her skin. Don't think about it! she told herself. Not now! Not here!

'How are you, Allysha?'

His voice—always deep—had the faintest American twang, giving it a mysterious appeal. She forced her head up and looked at him. Tightening her clasp on Peter's fingers, she said, 'I'm fine, thanks,' in the most offhand manner she could manage.

She turned to Peter and smiled brilliantly.

'I really must go and help Susan in the kitchen,' she murmured, loudly enough for Nick to hear. Another kiss, this one dropped on the hand that had held hers so comfortingly, then she released her grip and turned away—hurrying towards the kitchen as if her life depended on her immediate arrival there.

Susan was bustling between the refrigerator and the table, but Allysha soon realised that her mind wasn't entirely absorbed by her hostess duties.

'Have you and Peter been going out long?' she asked, indicating a laden tray that was ready to be taken outside.

Allysha paused and sighed inwardly. Her impulsive actions earlier, prompted by panic and shock, could lead her deeper and deeper into a distasteful deception.

'We're not really going out,' she said weakly, then wondered if the denial would only fuel Susan's interest. Helping Susan hadn't been the escape she needed! She picked up the tray and hurried out of the kitchen before the conversation could be continued.

Peter walked towards her as she passed the pool, and took the tray from her. Without anything to make her look busy or involved she felt lost and hesitated, unwilling to return to the kitchen and face further questions from Susan yet unable to mix and mingle with the other staff while Nick's presence among them set her nerves jangling and numbed her mind.

For six months she'd managed to avoid socialising with these people she liked and respected. Why, oh why, had she allowed Peter to persuade her to begin today of all days?

'Stick with me,' Peter suggested. 'I'll put this lot down and we'll both go back to the kitchen for another load.'

Allysha looked into his face and saw the kindness in his eyes—the silent promise to stand by her.

She gave a rueful smile.

'Careful!' she warned. 'You'll lose your chauvinistic, macho image altogether if you continue to be so perceptive and sympathetic.'

Peter winked at her.

'That wouldn't do at all,' he agreed. 'You'll have to promise to keep any kindness a closely guarded secret.'

As they drew closer to the small conversational groups in the shaded area Allysha was aware of Nick's presence among the guests, aware in a physical way so

that her skin tingled and grew cold in the summer heat
and her ears were alert for the deep, velvety tones of
his voice.

I'll have to leave Rainbow Bay! she decided, aware
that her physical reaction to the man had not disappeared in the past year. If anything, it had grown
stronger, more insistent, more invasive—penetrating
every cell of her body and filling them with a deep,
gnawing hunger.

She knew that it would be impossible to live with
such yearning, and felt a wave of anguish wash over
her. As she had grown in self-confidence and carefully
pieced together a new life for herself, she had also
grown to love the town of Rainbow Bay where her
healing process had begun.

'Come on, we're workers!' Peter said, and put an
arm around her shoulders to lead her back towards
the house.

'You want to tell me about it?' he asked when they
could no longer be overheard. 'We don't have to go
back into the kitchen and carry things. We could find
a quiet corner, I could get you a brandy, and we
could talk.'

Allysha shook her head.

'What I'd like to do is run away,' she admitted, 'but
I won't do that yet! And as for brandy—I'm on call
tonight. We'll help Susan, then eat and then maybe we
could leave. . .'

Peter gave her shoulders a friendly squeeze.

'That's no problem because I usually go early,' he
assured her. 'You'll have to put up with some sugges-
tive remarks and a good deal of teasing, but I reckon
you can cope with that.'

Puzzled by what sounded like admiration in the words, she looked at him.

He nodded in reply to the unspoken question.

'I don't know what happened between you and that fellow but, as far as I'm concerned, you're OK,' he said. 'A little intrigue won't hurt anyone on the staff, Allysha. In fact, those who notice will probably get a great deal of pleasure from it! So, if I can help by playing a part—if a bit of pretence will give you time to work out what's best for you—let's go with it.'

'Oh, Peter!' she whispered, husky-voiced with her gratitude. 'Thank you!'

'Not going out together, but billing and cooing at the bottom of my steps. Get in here and make yourselves useful,' Susan ordered.

They looked up at her and laughed.

'Billing and cooing, indeed!' Peter objected as he balanced another laden tray on his fingers. 'We were having a medical discussion, if you must know.'

Susan smiled knowingly and Allysha realised that, no matter what was said to deny it, their relationship was firmly established in at least one colleague's mind.

Peter stayed by her side, and his presence gave her the strength she needed to keep her rampaging emotions under control. Lachlan and Stewart Stone provided a further diversion. Dry and dressed, they claimed her as an old friend, insisting that she and Peter share the table they had chosen and introducing her to Leonie's children, Mitchell and Caroline.

'Mum told me there was a woman pilot at the Base,' Caroline said shyly. 'She's always telling me about good job opportunities for women.'

'Because you're stuck on the idea of being a nurse,'

Mitchell pointed out. 'And it's such a predictable job for a girl.'

'Predictable?' Lachlan argued. 'We had breakfast cereal for dinner five nights last week when Mum was called out or held up and didn't get home in time to cook.'

'Boys your age should be able to cook their own dinners!' Peter said severely, peeling away another layer of the distorted image of him Allysha had carried in her mind. She tried to concentrate on the casual conversation, ignoring the tremors that riffled across her skin and the taunting awareness that Nick was close by.

The twins were laughing uproariously at Peter's comment.

'They can both cook,' Caroline explained. 'They just try the poor-little-us-eating-breakfast-cereal routine to make people feel sorry for them. Mum falls for it all the time, although I don't know why because everyone knows breakfast cereals are very nutritious.'

There was an earnest innocence about Caroline, Allysha decided, and felt a pang of sympathy for the rebellious, angry, intransigent fourteen-year-old she had been. But you can't change the past, she reminded herself, and concentrated on removing a char-grilled prawn from a kebab stick.

The sharp shrill of a phone made them all pause and look around—too used to hearing the insistent summons to be able to ignore it.

Checking the movement within the group, Allysha realised that it was Jack who had answered and she watched his face as he spoke. Now that most places in their area came under a satellite network, phone consultations had taken over from the radio. It was more convenient in many ways and the people in isolated places enjoyed being able to phone their doctor, but it meant that consultations could take place in strange situations—anywhere from supermarket aisles to the bathroom.

But would this be a consultation or a call that needed a physical response?

'It's an evac,' Jack said as he slipped the phone back into his pocket. 'Who's on call?'

'I am, of course!' Susan responded. 'I worked out years ago it was easier to have a party when I was on call than when Eddie was. That way, he gets to clear up all the mess!'

'Well, that's bad luck for you because you don't have to come,' Jack told her. 'That was Helen Jensen at Castleford. She has a sick baby—high temp, rigid abdomen, obviously in pain and not responding to anti-biotics. She's wondering if it might be appendicitis.'

Jack was finishing his meal as he spoke, and Allysha ate another prawn. Who knew when they would eat again?

'I'll go in case the little chap needs an immediate operation, and Helen can assist me,' Jack explained, pushing back his chair and straightening up. 'You ready, Allysha?'

She picked up the handbag she had slung over the back of the chair and nodded, pleased to have a valid reason to escape the gathering. Maybe once she was alone at the controls of the plane—surrounded by the purple beauty and special serenity of the night sky—she could think rationally about Nick's sudden reappearance and make some sensible decisions about her future.

'I'll walk out with you,' Peter said, rising to stand beside her. The twins' goodbyes blotted out the conversation from Jack's table but, as she turned to wave a general farewell to the other staff, she saw Nick shaking hands and thanking Susan for inviting him.

'Might as well take the new boy along to show him something of our bit of Australia,' Jack explained cheerfully, and Allysha was grateful for Peter's supporting hand beneath her elbow.

'Perhaps it's best to get this reunion over and done with,' Peter whispered as they followed the two men through the garden. 'Just keep your chin up and remember you have an adoring lover in me. What more could any woman want?'

He was trying to cheer her up, and she responded with a semblance of a smile.

'Maybe the ability to dematerialise, or to vanish in a puff of purple smoke?' she suggested as they crossed the footpath towards Jack's car. She watched Nick bend forward to open the front, passenger-side door.

'You don't need to do that,' Peter assured her, his hand tightening on her elbow as she approached the new doctor.

She looked at Nick and wondered, but his expression was unreadable. Whatever emotion he might be feeling was hidden behind a stern, unsmiling mask. Or perhaps there wasn't any emotion to hide! Perhaps he had meant what he'd said twelve months ago when he'd told her that he would not put up with her antics any longer—that she had killed his love for her, and their engagement was off.

'Have a good trip,' Peter said.

She sank bonelessly into the front seat, all strength consumed by the catastrophic memory. He leant into the car and kissed her on the lips, but her skin was too cold to register the gentle salute. Behind her a car door slammed sharply, then Peter was straightening up. He closed her door and she was shut into a metal prison with a man who hated her.

'Here we go again!' Jack said cheerfully, taking his place behind the wheel and starting the engine. He seemed totally oblivious to the atmospheric conditions that were battering Allysha. To him it was just another night, another emergency call!

She straightened in her seat, calling into force all the professionalism she had learned from her workmates over the previous six months. She, also, had a job to do. Time enough to worry about Nick when the mission was successfully completed.

'If you operate out there, will you bring the child back to the Bay?' she asked Jack, hoping that she sounded more composed than she was.

'I'll have to wait and see,' he told her. 'We'll take a paediatric bag and a humidicrib. He's three months old, but might fit in one if he's small for his age. If we have to bring him back I'd rather have him in a controlled atmosphere than have to fool around humidifying the oxygen and keeping his temperature stable with wrappings.'

Allysha nodded. Usually the flight sisters took charge of equipment, but she preferred to stow it in the plane herself to ensure that nothing would come loose if they hit turbulence. Knowing which bulky items they were taking made it easier for her to decide what to put where. She could also help by getting equipment out of the storage lockers while Jack decided and packed what drugs he would take.

'Castleford has a hospital, you said?'

Nick's voice caused shivers along her spine.

'A small one,' Jack confirmed. 'Helen Jensen is the sister in charge.'

'And a theatre? You'd be happy operating there?'

Listening to his questions, Allysha remembered Nick's persistence—his determination to learn as much as he could about anything, whether it was sheep drenching or the mechanics of flying!

'I'd be happy to perform simple surgery at any of the small hospitals,' Jack explained. 'Over the years their equipment has been updated as much as possible and, at Castleford in particular, it is kept in pristine condition.'

'Sister Jensen sounds like a perfectionist,' Nick remarked and Allysha heard Jack chuckle.

'She's renowned throughout the north,' Jack admitted. 'I've seen grown men quake in front of her when she spots a bit of dirt intruding into her hospital on a carelessly scraped boot. She's been at Castleford for as long as most people can remember, sometimes on her own and sometimes with staff. At the moment she has two nurse aides and a cook of sorts.'

'Of sorts?' queried Nick.

'Actually, he's a terrific cook,' Allysha explained, pleased she was calm enough to join in the general conversation. 'As long as you strike him on a good day.'

'Bert Grimes, the cook, is an alcoholic,' Jack added. 'Goes for months without a drink, then bang—he's back on the grog and out of his mind for about a fortnight.'

They were getting closer to the airport, and Allysha felt the thrill of an imminent departure ease the tension in her muscles. Flying was like a drug to her—like drink must be to old Bert, she decided. At least when she was in control of the plane she could forget everything else, escaping into her own encapsulated world.

'A flight to Castleford while old Bert's on the booze is an experience to remember,' Jack said, turning the car onto the side road that ran along the perimeter fence. 'His DTs follow the classic pattern—right down to seeing pink elephants around his bed at night, and voices telling him to do the strangest things.'

'Like jump off the roof of the hotel,' Allysha recalled. Her self-control had reasserted itself and she was able to act as if nothing was worrying her. Nick hadn't seen through her anger to the pain when she'd accepted his decision to break off their engagement twelve months ago—so why should he suspect that she was acting now?

They drew up outside the hangar and she was first out of the car, crossing to speak to Jeff Yates, the mechanic, who—alerted by Jack before they left the party—had come straight to the airport and wheeled the plane out onto the apron.

'It's Castleford, and we might be on the ground there for a while so you go home—we'll put it away,' she told him, hurrying on into the tiny office to draw up a flight plan and fax it through to the civil aviation authorities.

She began pre-flight checks, circling the plane, and then as Jack and Nick carried the medical gear into the cabin she followed them on board and stowed it carefully, checking the doorlock before moving to her seat in the cockpit.

'Nice moonlit night,' she heard Jack say. 'You want to sit up front and see the beauty of the tropical north?'

She didn't hear Nick's reply, but knew it had been an assent when he dropped into the seat beside her.

Waves of awareness washed across her skin, and she found it increasingly difficult to focus on the complicated procedures of departure.

He was so close that she fancied she could feel him breathing. She remembered other times he'd sat beside her in a plane—in her own little Cessna, a twin of Eddie's—flying to the Barossa Valley for a stolen weekend of pleasure—of wine-tasting and being tourists.

Back then she had been shaking with anticipatory pleasure, wanting him so much that she didn't know how she was going to manage the flight. She had been embarrassed by the heat he had kindled in a body she'd believed too cold for physical desire, and frightened by the turbulent emotion she had felt in a heart she'd thought too cynical for love.

She turned the plane for take-off and accelerated. Coming home had been different, she remembered as the increasing speed pressed her back into her seat. Sated with love and lost in the wonderment of feelings she could not identify, she had flown home in a dream of for ever and ever—a dream that took six months' harsh reality to tarnish, and Nick's blunt pronouncement that it was over to finally kill.

'And is work your latest enthusiasm? Another little game to while away the tedium of a self-indulgent life?' he asked, the noise of the engines almost drowning out his words as they lifted into the night sky.

Allysha turned to look at him, startled by the bitterness in his voice, then shifted her attention quickly back to her instrument panel.

He had looked at her with love—that other time! A love so vibrant, so passionate, so intense that it had frightened her! And, frightened, she had shied away,

played the fool and teased him for his sober
dedication. . .

'What's the ETA?'

Jack's voice interrupted her thoughts before she
found words to answer Nick's question and reminded
her that pilots were supposed to keep one hundred per
cent of their minds on their jobs, particularly during
the climb to cruising altitude.

'Ten-thirty,' she told him. 'The weather's clear
ahead, and I think Castleford has the new solar-powered
flares so landing shouldn't be any problem.'

'I'm going to try to get on to Helen now,' he said.
'I'll let them know.'

She heard Jack speaking again, but couldn't distin-
guish the words. Beside her, Nick was looking out
through the side window but the disapproval which had
been evident in his words was pulsing from his body
in unremitting waves.

I won't be able to work with him, she thought, and
felt a strange moisture haze her eyes. She'd worked
hard to fill the emptiness and banish the pain when
he'd walked out of her life. Cutting herself off from
the old crowd of pleasure-seekers, she had turned to
flying—taking extra lessons and enduring long hours
of practice in the air. In the beginning it had been
to escape her misery, something to pass the time, but
gradually learning the advanced skills of a commercial
pilot had become an end in itself.

Upgrading her pilot's licence became the goal, and
once she'd achieved it she could apply for a real job.
Had it been fate that decreed she was eventually
employed by the Flying Doctors, or had she been clinging to a shred of memory and subconsciously directed
her endeavours that way?

'Where I was in America there were always lights beneath the plane.'

Nick's voice broke the silence in the cockpit—and the bitterness was gone from its deep tones.

'Sometimes strung out along a highway, marking a small town or clustered at an intersection but, more often, lights from houses, linked together along roads with sprinkles of small towns and villages splashing yellow into the surrounding darkness.'

Allysha swallowed.

He had always painted pictures with his words, and she could see the jewel-bright towns as clearly as if they were spread beneath her on the velvety dark plains of the outback.

'Did you enjoy your stay there?' she asked, and silently congratulated herself on sounding composed when other, more insistent questions were hammering in her head. Like—did you fall in love with someone else? Get married? Or engaged again? Did you break another heart? Or hundreds? Or are other women less affected than me by your strange self-containment? Your silent appeal? Your body's magnetism?

Allysha was shivering by the time he answered so his casual reply, 'Not particularly!' barely registered at first.

And when it did, she found that she couldn't ask the next question—the obvious, 'Why not?', because she didn't want to know the answer.

The radio demanded her attention, another call for Jack but this time patched through from the Base. She switched it to the cabin receiver, and caught the name Herd Island.

'Have you enjoyed your stay in the north?' Nick asked when she was free of distractions.

She glanced at him, but his face looked as uncaring about her reply as his voice had been.

'Yes, I have,' she said defiantly. 'I have enjoyed it thoroughly, and I shall continue to enjoy it for many years to come!'

It was the old bravado she had used as a protective shield from childhood—a defiant, so-what attitude with which she'd faced the world. It had surged back into being when she'd kissed Peter by the pool, and now she knew that it would be her only defence in this new, untenable situation. To let Nick see her despair, her confusion and her pain would be more humiliating than she could bear.

She ordered her straining muscles to relax, and added, 'After all, Peter's committed to the Service, and I wouldn't want to disrupt his career plans.'

CHAPTER THREE

THE words were like the tiny, poison-tipped arrows the Amazonian Indians used in their blowpipes, Nick decided. And every one found its target in his heart and spread its poison through his body.

And how dared Allysha talk about disrupting her latest victim's career in the RFDS? She'd done little else to his career from the moment they'd met! And not only his career! She'd successfully disrupted his thoughts, disrupted his feelings, disrupted his body, disrupted his sleep, disrupted his life!

He sneaked a sideways look towards her, as if an unemotional appraisal might explain the potential for disaster that was packed into her slight, attractive but not stunning, five feet four of womanhood.

She was hunched slightly forward in her seat, frowning over her instruments, and the little tip tilt to her nose, the tiny imperfection she tried to deny, was practically twitching with concentration.

'I'm dropping down,' she told him, oblivious of his scrutiny. 'As we get closer you should see the lights.'

'Always providing you're heading in the right direction,' he gibed, remembering a story she had told him about an early flight she'd once made over the Channel Country in flood time when she'd been unable to find the river she'd counted on as a guide.

She didn't spare him a glance, but continued to concentrate on her instruments as she answered.

'We have GPS, or Global Positioning System, on all

the aircraft now. Once we know the latitude and longi-
tude to the strips it cuts out a lot of navigational work
and does away with ground identification points
altogether.'

Now she turned, and actually smiled at him—a tight
little effort, to be sure, but definitely recognisable as
a smile.

'But I still feel reassured when I see the flares
where the GPS tells me they should be. I find atomic
clocks in satellites and multiple signals bouncing
around at the speed of light as hard to accept as fairy
tales.'

'Well, your flares are dead ahead, so something
worked.'

He spoke abruptly, even harshly, but her mention of
fairy tales had reminded him. . .

'Allysha, can we do Herd Island after this?'

The urgency in Jack's voice alerted them both to a
new crisis.

'It shouldn't be a problem,' Allysha said. 'I'll work
out fuel and a new flight plan as soon as we've landed.
Is it urgent? Will you forget about operating here and
simply evacuate the child and mother? Do you want a
quick turn-around?'

She welcomed the diversion. Nick's presence by her
side had been intruding more and more into her
thoughts, and distracting her body with its potent fam-
iliarity.

'I'll have to examine the child before I decide. If he
can be left for another two hours, we'll take him.
There's a fellow on Herd shoved a screwdriver into a
generator or something equally irrational. He's had an
electric shock and is badly burnt as well. He'll need
specialist care as quickly as possible.'

Nick turned in his seat, as if to ask something, but Jack hadn't finished issuing orders.

'If I operate at Castleford, Helen Jensen can assist. Nick, could you stay here at the airstrip and help Allysha with the fuel? That way, we'll be ready to go as soon as I return. According to Helen, old Bert's on a bender so he won't be out to lend a hand.'

'All strapped in?' Allysha asked before Nick had time to agree. 'There's a vehicle by the strip; let's hope they've driven along it to chase off any roos or buffalo. I'll fly over once to make sure, so keep your eyes peeled.'

She brought the plane in for a quick swoop, pleased there was bitumen on this particular strip. She could use her flaps to brake more quickly without throwing up loose stones and other debris which damaged the aircraft's paintwork and outer shell. Landings on unsurfaced strips were always far more wary, and consequently much slower, procedures.

The plane touched down gently, bounced once and then settled, engines roaring as she slowed it to a walking pace before turning and taxiing back towards the vehicle and tiny storage shed where their fuel supplies were kept.

Jack was first out, his emergency equipment bag slung on his back and the smaller paediatric bag in one hand.

'See you later,' he called as he dashed across to the waiting car. In the darkness Allysha couldn't identify the chauffeur. With no policeman stationed at Castleford, anyone from the publican to the local schoolteacher could be called upon to meet their plane.

Nick had left his seat by the time Allysha had shut down the engines. He was waiting in the shadowy cabin, dimly lit by battery-operated lights while they were on the ground.

'Fuel's in a small shed at the edge of the field,' she told him briskly, trying to reinforce her professional image. 'I can handle the refuelling on my own, if you'd prefer to wait here.'

She brushed past him, wanting to be out of the confined space—out of the orbit of his magnetism.

'And this is the girl who would sit in service stations, tapping her long fingernails on the steering-wheel until someone came to top up the tank of her dinky little Porsche?'

Allysha flinched at the memory but there was a fleeting suggestion of humour in Nick's words, not the bitterness she thought she'd heard earlier. She shrugged, uneasily aware she would prefer anger. She could handle her own feelings more easily when he was antagonistic.

'This is different,' she pointed out. 'The staff in service stations are paid to attend to customers' needs, just as I'm paid to refuel my plane.'

She stomped off towards the shed, hoping that he would make her prove her point and not follow and offer to help.

'How do you get the drums over to the plane?'

Futile hope!

'I have a pneumatic-lift trolley. The drums are stored on chocks and I can roll the forks of the trolley in underneath, lift them up and push them out onto the tarmac.'

She unlocked the shed and manoeuvred the trolley into position under one of the full drums.

'Labour-saving devices now there's a woman on the team?' he asked, and the anger he'd failed to provoke

with his remark about her past behaviour flamed to
fever-pitch.

'It makes sense for all the pilots,' she said, forcing
the words out from between clenched teeth. 'The
Service can't afford to be paying workers' compen-
sation to pilots who've ruptured themselves or injured
their backs manhandling fuel drums.'

He didn't reply and she took the opportunity to add,
'And I notice none of the male doctors are complaining
about the plan to introduce hoists into the planes or
pretending they are only for the women on the staff.'

'I stand corrected,' Nick said, then moved her gently
but firmly out of the way and took over the handle of
the trolley, pulling it, now loaded with two drums, out
of the hut and turning it in the direction of the plane.

His touch paralysed her, and she could neither object
nor follow.

He can't still affect me like this! she told herself.
It's the effect of seeing him again after all this time.
It's shock.

But her insides quivered with remembered delight
and her breasts ached with a frustrated yearning, too
long denied.

One heavy sigh, then she lifted the hand-pump from
its place on the wall, unwrapped the greasy, protective
cloth that kept it free from dust and followed Nick
towards the plane.

'One drum or two here?' he asked as she fitted the
pump into the drum, then ran the hose up towards the
fuel inlet valve.

'One for each wing. We'd get home on what we've
got but, with the humidity at this time of the year, if we
carry excess airspace we risk water from condensation
mixing with the fuel,' she explained. She clambered up

onto the wing and fed the line into the starboard tank. If she concentrated on work maybe she could forget what Nick's presence was doing to her body!

Nick looked at her, skin silvered by the moon, determination and pride stiffening every sinew of that delectable body. He felt proud of her, he decided, then inwardly scoffed at the ridiculous thought.

The Allysha Craig he'd known had inherited about a quarter of far western New South Wales. She'd been the spoiled darling of the social set, the immaculately groomed, expensively dressed butterfly who had demanded—and received, he had to admit—attention and adoration wherever she went. She'd been sharp-witted—and often sharp-tongued—and totally oblivious of all life beyond her narrow, exclusive world.

Could that Allysha have turned into a dedicated career woman?

The idea would have been laughable if it hadn't been so ridiculous!

No, he decided. She was here because of that man—Peter whoever he was! He groaned inwardly. Peter was certainly good-looking enough to turn any woman's head, but had he turned Allysha's to the extent that she was seriously trying to change her ways? Did she love him enough to have turned her back on her reckless, feckless friends and indulgent, irresponsible lifestyle?

The thought made him feel physically sick and he began to wonder how disappointed Jack Gregory would be if he had to get another new doctor before his latest recruit had started work.

'That's one done!'

Allysha's voice brought him out of his gloomy thoughts and he turned towards her. She was back on the ground, intent on lifting the pump clear of the empty

drum. She looked like a sprite—an illustration of some
hard-working imp or helpful elf from a children's
book—so delicately formed, so fragile-seeming in the
mystic moonlight.

'I'll wheel the second drum across to the other side,'
he said gruffly, then thought she'd flinched away from
him as if the words had slapped against her skin.

She filled the second tank, and he offered to take the
empty drums back to the shed.

'And I'll contact Base and find out what's happening,
both here and at Herd Island,' Allysha said.

She moved quickly and he fancied that she was
escaping, but that was a stupid assumption. She might
have felt slightly awkward, meeting up with him again,
but if that unfairly handsome doctor back in Rainbow
Bay had been responsible for the change in her person-
ality she must be secure enough in his love to cope
with an old fiancé's sudden reappearance.

'None of which makes me feel any better!' he muttered to himself, pushing the empty drums and the
trolley into the shed and shutting the door. He was
snapping the padlock into its hasp when he heard her
calling.

'Could you take the radio, Nick?' she asked, racing
across the tarmac towards him. 'Jack's operating on the
baby, and the nurse at Herd Island is concerned about
her electric-shock victim. She says she has two large-
bore IVs running with Ringer's and has inserted a Foley
catheter, but is worried about his heart, as well as his
urinary output and the possibility of renal failure.'

He took her arm and they hurried back to the plane.

'Did she say anything about the burn injuries?' he
asked, taking the steps two at a time.

'She said it was a hand-to-foot current pathway and

something about muscle damage and some cardiac
effect but no apparent respiratory damage, although she
has him on oxygen.'

She reached into the cockpit and pulled the hand
mike towards her.

'Hello, Herd. I'm passing you to Nick Furlong, the
new Base doctor,' she said. 'I'll hand over now.'

Nick took the receiver from her hand, noticing how
steady her fingers were and wondering again at the
evidence of this new sensible, capable and responsible
Allysha.

But she'd always been capable, he reminded himself.
Capable of getting into more trouble than any proverbial
cartload of monkeys.

He dragged his mind out of the past and listened to
the nurse at Herd Island explaining her problem.

'You've protected the patient's spine and immobil-
ised his head,' he repeated. 'You've an airway in place
and his breathing sounds are bilateral and you've
infusion going. Tachycardia? I suppose that's to be
expected. Pain relief?'

Nick listened, then said, 'ECG changes?

'Inferior MI?' he asked and Allysha, watching him,
could see the concentrated effort of his thoughts.

'An electric current, especially one from hand to foot,
can bypass the respiratory centre but cause damage
to the heart muscle. Electricity takes the line of least
resistance and collects at the grounding point. With
alternating current there's a likelihood of chest muscle
contractions, which could cause fibrillation. I'd try IV
NTG. Jack's due back at the plane any moment and the
pilot tells me we're only half an hour's flight from you.'

He handed the mike back to Allysha, who added,
'I'll radio Base an ETA as soon as we're airborne and

they'll contact you. If you need to speak to a doctor in the meantime, Base will patch you through.'

Allysha was sorry when the conversation concluded. While she thought about work she could forget the tantalising agony of Nick's closeness; forget that he was Nick and pretend that he was just another professional, working with her—often against impossible odds. She peered out into the darkness, seeking an escape from an attraction she suspected was completely one-sided.

Hadn't she tried to tempt him into bed after he'd made his damning assessment of her character and ended it with his final announcement? Hadn't she almost prostituted herself, her pride momentarily crushed beneath the horror of his bitter words?

Her cheeks grew hot at the recollection of that day— of her behaviour! When her foolish teasing had failed to tempt him, she'd shrugged and pretended she hadn't cared; pretended it had been purely a physical affair, sanctioned in his prudish eyes by an engagement ring.

She'd handed back the ring with a casual flick of her wrist and an insincere smile, while her heart had shrivelled to a cold, icy lump. She had behaved exactly as he'd expected her to behave, but it had been to hide a pain so deep she'd wondered if she could survive it!

'Headlights approaching.'

His voice, still hauntingly familiar in her ears, made her steady herself and sweep away the tattered flags of her old, faded dreams.

'I'll close the door and start the engines, then taxi to the end and turn for take-off. Jack's driver will bring him to the plane.'

Nick sank into one of the cabin seats, and she was glad he wasn't beside her to witness the unsteadiness of her fingers as they went through their routine movements.

This gave the word 'autopilot' a whole new meaning, she decided, knowing that it was training and practice carrying her through the procedures of taxiing and turning while her mind and body rioted at will.

'Are you there, Allysha?'

Jack's voice echoed from the radio and she frowned as she acknowledged his call.

'I'm held up at the hospital,' he said. 'It was a twisted appendix and a nasty operation, so I want the little fellow conscious and stable before I move him. Could you fly Nick to Herd, collect the other patient and come back for me?'

The headlights had tracked to the far end of the runway, where the vehicle had turned awkwardly and was now accelerating towards them. Something in the determination of the lights' peculiar progress distracted her.

'Allysha?'

'Sorry, Jack, there's a vehicle on the runway. We saw the lights and thought it was you returning. I'm at the eastern end and ready for take-off. The vehicle is gathering speed as it heads towards us.'

She watched the swerving progress of the unknown conveyance with a growing concern.

'It's not going to stop, so I'll have to move.'

She dropped the mike and released the brakes, gathering momentum as they approached the intruder. Nick loomed behind her in the cockpit, peering out into the night.

'He's veering more frequently to the left, isn't he?' she asked him, her mind absorbed by the task ahead of her.

'I'd say so,' he agreed doubtfully. 'But why don't we wait for him to come up to us? How do you know it isn't someone driving out with a message or a patient?'

'Because vehicles aren't allowed on the strip while we're on it. They can drive along it before we land to clear animals or come out with fuel, but once we're moving it's our space. If he had a message or a patient all he has to do is stop by the side of the runway and blink his lights, and he has made no effort to do that.'

'But what on earth are you doing? Why are you accelerating towards him?'

Good questions, Allysha thought, but instinct had told her to move and she had moved.

'The plane's not manoeuvrable enough to swerve around him if he does continue to come at us, so I'm going to take off over him,' she said, gritting her teeth as her mind ran through the procedures she'd need to employ. 'If I get it right we should make it safely. Sit down and strap in.'

He dropped into the seat beside her.

'And if you don't?' he asked as he clicked his seat belt fastening.

She felt like smiling! There was no panic in Nick's voice, simply an academic interest in the outcome.

'If I don't we'll probably hit him, but as he would have hit us if I'd stayed where we were we won't be much worse off.'

She concentrated on the advancing lights, letting her fingers meld with the plane so that every movement would be smoothly co-ordinated.

The headlights grew bigger and bigger as they accelerated remorselessly towards them, brightening the cockpit with their distracting glare. Allysha felt the engines throbbing, building to a crescendo of power that strained for release.

'Now!' she breathed when it seemed that they must surely collide with the intruder, and her hands obeyed her brain's command. She dropped the flaps another notch to get extra lift.

'As long as he can't go any faster we'll beat him,' she said as confidence in her ability brought its own boost of adrenalin soaring through her veins.

She knew she'd sucked in air and imagined she'd heard an indrawn breath from Nick, but there was no time to reconsider. Willing herself to succeed, she pulled the yoke hard towards her body, holding it against the protesting shoulders and screaming whine of the engine and then, what seemed like an aeon later, she felt the plane lift.

'Not too steep, my beauty,' she murmured, easing back a little. 'Ten feet should clear it, fifteen to be safe.

'Not too steep, not too steep,' she repeated to herself, steadying the plane against the extra drag. They lifted, engines roaring with the effort. Blackness filled their eyes as the headlights disappeared beneath them. Allysha closed her eyes in a silent prayer and brought the plane to a more reasonable angle of ascent, carefully bringing the flaps back up and adjusting the trim.

'Didn't we use steep climbs to practise stalling?' Nick asked, and now she allowed herself to smile.

'We did,' she agreed, grinning with relief. 'But if ever you're practising it again, remember to do it at altitude and not on take-off.'

'You're over the trees,' Nick said, and she released the pent-up air from her lungs, then fixed the direction-finder on the GPS and reached for the radio mike.

'We're up, Jack,' she said, 'but could you rustle up

a posse of some kind and send them out to the airfield
to get rid of the maniac out there? I took off over
him OK, but I wouldn't like to have to dodge him on
landing.'

She heard Jack agree and signed off, then called Herd
to let them know she was on the way.

'This is a ridiculous job for you!' Nick grumbled
when she'd finished with business and relaxed for a
moment before she had to think about the next landing.
'I can't believe that fellow approves of your doing it.'

Allysha shrugged. She wasn't going to defend herself
or her job to Nick.

'Or is that why you're doing it?' he persisted. 'To
annoy him? To drive him insane with worry over what
antics you might perform next?'

Is that how he really saw her? So shallow that she
would take on a job like this for a whim? She didn't
know whether to feel sad or angry, but decided angry
was easier and safer. And, on second thoughts, maybe
she would defend herself!

'I have a seriously injured patient waiting at Herd
Island, and a baby to be evacuated from Castleford.
That was not an antic but a professionally judged
manoeuvre to keep the plane safe so I can airlift those
two people back to medical attention in Rainbow Bay.'

She spoke coldly, the tiny bubble of pride she'd felt
in pulling off the tricky take-off pricked by his
contempt.

'Hmm!' he snorted, and she turned to see him glaring
ferociously at her.

She glared back, then thought how stupid they must
look—if an unseen watcher was peering through the
windows! She let the anger go, relaxing back into
the seat.

'Scared you, did I?' she asked, thinking fear might explain his reaction.

'Scared me stiff,' he admitted, shaking his head at the admission. 'Not that I ever doubted you could do it! You always could fly better than most people drive.'

Allysha squirmed at the unexpected praise, reluctantly given, but was pleased when a stutter from the radio heralded further communication. She couldn't let Nick sneak in under her guard with easy compliments.

'That's Katie, the Base radio officer,' she told Nick as she recognised the voice. 'We're coming in to land at Herd; could you acknowledge and see what she wants? Surely not another emergency!'

He had handled radio communications at Broken Hill and would know what to do, but as he picked up the mike in his slim fingers her heart contracted and she had to will her hand to remain on the controls although it ached with the need to fold over his—just once more!

Night lights at Herd were always makeshift, but the strip was well-packed antbed, and firm for landings and take-offs. Tonight light was provided by a truck of some kind, headlights on high beam and pointing down the runway. At the far end another vehicle—she suspected it was the decrepit old station-wagon they used as an ambulance—was parked with its tail and brake lights glowing red.

She brought the plane around so that it was lined up above the truck. The headlights would give her a guide for touching down, while the red lights at the other end would keep her straight without blinding her—as headlights could. She concentrated on the task of landing the plane safely, so absorbed that she was unaware of Nick's conversation until they were drawing to a standstill.

'It seems Katie went back to Base when we left the barbecue because she knew you'd be out of phone range. She couldn't patch Jack through once we were airborne again, but she said to tell you they were at the landing strip and had Bert under control.'

'It was Bert?' Allysha asked, easing the plane to a halt and putting on the brakes.

'Apparently!' Nick confirmed as he unbuckled his seat belt. 'It seems he thought he was in a plane and was taxiing for take-off when you came thundering down towards him and nearly gave the poor man a heart attack.'

'So he might not have been planning to hit us,' she admitted as she followed him into the cabin of the plane.

'Maybe not planning it, but the way he was going he would have run into the plane if you hadn't taken evasive action.' He gave a little smile that made her heart lurch.

'I don't think the truck would have lifted off the ground in time to miss us!' he added, his smile broadening at the silly joke. 'It seems you gave him such a fright when you took off over him that he stalled the engine and couldn't remember how to get it started again. As well as saving the plane, you probably saved him from a serious accident.'

I suppose that's some consolation, Allysha thought but, as she watched Nick tread lightly down the steps and greet the approaching party, she knew she wanted more.

I can't work with him, her heart cried. Not while I still feel as I do! How can I hide those feelings every day?

She stepped back as two efficient bearers pushed a stretcher into the plane.

'And Sister said to remind you that it's her stretcher. She knows you won't want to risk transferring him again, but said remember to bring it back next time you're out this way,' one of the men warned.

Allysha smiled and assured them that she would see it came back. Trying to keep track of equipment was a nightmare, especially as this stretcher was likely to end up at Rainbow Bay hospital. They introduced themselves to their sleepy patient.

'Do you want to examine him before we take off again?' she asked Nick.

He was hanging the infusion bag on the track above the stretcher while she fixed it in place.

'I'll connect him to our monitor, and strap in here beside him. It's such a short hop I'll do what I can, but I think the main assessment will be done on the trip home from Castleford.'

He dropped into the seat beside the stretcher as he spoke and she shut the door and slipped past him, intent on carrying out her part of the mission as expertly as the medical team would performs theirs.

Jack was waiting at Castleford. As soon as the plane was stationary he hurried towards them, his equipment bags banging against his legs. He was followed by another person and, as Allysha came down the steps to help, she saw it was a woman, carrying a baby.

'Well, you've had a bit of fun from what I hear,' Jack said, passing her one of the bags and turning to help the young mother into the plane. She strapped into one of the seats in the rear and Allysha stowed the bag, then handed her new passenger a small pillow to help make the baby comfortable on her lap.

She heard Nick ask a question.

'The operation was more complicated than I'd expected,' Jack replied. 'I'm concerned about the effect on the bowel and thought it was best to have the little fellow in hospital until we're certain it's working properly. As you can see, he won't fit in our crib.'

She turned to look at the large, healthy-looking baby asleep in his mother's arms, and smiled. He looked more like a six-month-old child and certainly wouldn't have fitted in their life-saving capsule. She closed the door and secured the lock.

'Now,' Jack said to Nick, 'tell me about your man.'

Nick explained about the tachycardia and peeled back the loose dressing on the man's left foot.

'His hand's badly burned, but I think the exit wound will prove worse. The alternating current of the generator has caused an explosive force and extensive tissue necrosis.'

Another night, another flight! Allysha thought, shuddering at the description of the man's injuries. She walked past them to the cockpit and started the engines. The patients might differ, their injuries or illnesses might be more or less serious, but to the staff of the RFDS it was all part of the job.

Only now it was different! she acknowledged as the ground slid away from beneath them, and the dark shadows that were trees grew smaller and smaller.

She radioed Katie that they were airborne and gave her their ETA at Rainbow Bay, so that she could alert the ambulance. With the autopilot locked in on their destination she relaxed, trying to recapture the magic of the starlit night. But the beauty of it all was lost to her as her mind waged war with itself.

I can't stay, one part of it proclaimed, while the opposition argued that by leaving she would prove herself to be as irresponsible and flighty as Nick had always thought her. And since I refuse to do that! her determination announced, I'll have to stay!

'You did well earlier.' Jack slipped into the co-pilot's seat. 'The way Bert was he'd have hit the plane before he realised it was there.'

She smiled, grateful, in her muddled state, for the vote of confidence.

'I want to go up to the hospital,' he continued. 'I'll have to explain about the baby, and make sure the mother can be accommodated there.'

Allysha remembered her first impression of the passengers. The young woman had looked clean and tidy, but there'd been a suggestion of poverty in the much-washed cotton dress and her brown sandals had a scuffed, worn look.

'Lucia's Aunt Steph has started taking in relatives of patients,' she reminded Jack. 'And she doesn't charge board. She says the ones who can afford board usually stay at a hotel, and all she wants to do is help out— not make money out of other people's misfortune.'

She made a mental note to call in and see the woman the staff all knew as Aunt Steph. When her niece had left the Service to fly to France with Matt Laurant Aunt Steph had appointed herself chief hospital visitor and general support person for RFDS patients, and Allysha had become her ally, providing clothes and money for other little luxuries like perfumed soap and shampoo. Aunt Steph told her visitors that her niece had left the things behind and would beg them to take the clothes, and use the fragrant toiletries.

'I'll send her there if the hospital can't give her a bed,' Jack said, breaking into her thoughts. 'I'm certain they'll find somewhere for her for what's left of tonight.

Now, if I go in the ambulance, would you drive Nick home in my car? He's staying with me at the moment while he looks around for accommodation, although you couldn't get a handier place for a flat than The Bay Towers.'

Allysha made a feeble sound that she hoped sounded like agreement. She had rented a flat in the complex because it was close to the beach, not far from the Base and the airport, and had magnificent views across the bay. She had been living there for a month before she discovered that Jack had an apartment on a higher floor.

If Nick moved into the same building would she need to see any more of him than she did of Jack? If the thought of working with him was bad how much worse would accidental meetings in the lift be? Meetings she hadn't had time to prepare for? Her stomach scrunched at the thought.

Jack was explaining that Nick had only arrived the previous day and would not know his way around, but Allysha couldn't concentrate on his conversation. She was wondering why the thought of leaving, the thought now dominating her silent argument, made her feel so sad and empty.

CHAPTER FOUR

WHILE the patients were being loaded into the ambulance Allysha unlocked the hangar and steered the little electric dolly out onto the apron. She had hitched it to the plane for the tow back to the hangar before the ambulance departed. Once the plane was ready to move she climbed back into the cabin, tidying it up before she shut the door on it for the night. She took the bags of drugs and the equipment they hadn't used out with her, putting them onto the tray of the towing device.

'Does the doctor often go off in the ambulance?' Nick asked as she started the engine.

Asked or demanded? What's eating him now? she wondered.

'Not often,' she said shortly, then started off, manoeuvring her aircraft carefully into its place in the hangar.

He caught up with her as she unhitched the hook from the plane.

'It's dangerous for a woman to be hanging about these deserted places in the early hours of the morning!' he muttered, glaring at her again as if her very presence was an aggravation he could barely tolerate.

'It's no more dangerous for a woman than a man,' she argued. 'Wherever drugs might be stored there's an element of risk, although, here at Rainbow Bay, there's never been any trouble.'

'Well, I don't like it,' he growled, following her as she carried the bags across to the storage cabinets.

'Well, that's too bad,' she snapped, infuriated by his irrational concern, 'because it's none of your damn business!'

What was a gunshot wound or a bashing? Physical things that either killed you or could be healed. It was the invisible wounds that hurt for ever—wounds inflicted by words and actions—she knew that now. He had hurt her far more than any crazed drug addict could, and he hadn't cared about that!

She removed the cool-boxes to return them to the refrigerator, shoved the bags in forcefully and then locked the cupboards, knowing that she had to get away from him before her flimsy hold on self-control disintegrated.

As she spun around she saw his face, and realised that he was looking at her in a puzzled way. Something in that intent regard caught at her breath and she hesitated for an instant.

His hands lifted, as if to touch her, then a cheery voice called out, 'All OK? You lot locking up now?'

He turned away, releasing her from the spell.

'All OK, Bob,' she echoed, and waved her hand to the uniformed security man who stood in the doorway. 'We'll be on our way home in a few minutes.'

'Airport Security see us land, and they always drive over to the hangar to keep an eye out for any trouble,' she added coolly to Nick. 'Does that reassure you?'

He frowned at her, the moment when his look had held something else safely killed by the interruption.

'Come on,' she suggested, after she'd stowed the rest of the gear, 'I'll introduce you to Bob now. You'll meet all the security staff in time.'

But, as Nick followed her out of the hangar, the physical awareness she had managed to ignore while she concentrated on her job returned, and she felt it tugging insistently at her senses.

'We might be the only people left in the world,' he said quietly, as she drove out of the airport and turned onto the deserted road that led into the town.

Allysha understood what he was saying, having often felt that 'aloneness' as she travelled back to her flat in the early hours of the morning. If an atom bomb wiped out all the world but you and someone else, who would you choose for the someone else?

The old teaser from her teenage years came into her head—years when she'd finally gone to school, but only to be 'finished' at a small, select establishment for the daughters of the wealthy. Prince Albert of Monaco, Tom Cruise, their answers had been, but she knew—if she'd had the gift of foresight—her answer would always have been Nick.

'Did Jack tell you I'm staying with him until I find suitable accommodation?'

The question startled her out of the fragment of an impossible dream.

'Yes,' she replied, turning into the road that ran down to the Esplanade and The Bay Towers.

The waters of the bay shone like liquid mercury, and the curving arm of the protective headland looked black against their lightness. She heard Nick draw in his breath at the unexpected beauty, and saw his head turn towards her to share his wonder.

To share and, in sharing a precious moment, to intensify its impact, to make it more beautiful, more memorable, more real and meaningful.

Damn him! she thought, her insides churning with emotion. She pulled up at the security barrier and thrust Jack's card angrily into the control box while her mind continued its silent condemnation.

He taught me to see the wonders of nature, to stop in my frenetic race through life and take the time to look at things, to appreciate what was around me. Then he walked away and left me to look at it all alone—a punishment far worse than never having seen it.

The silence between them, thickened by her unspoken rage, was almost unbearable but she couldn't let him know her bitter despair and knew he would sense it if she tried to talk.

She parked the car and led the way to the lift, but as they waited for her summons to be answered she felt her anger drain away, replaced—again—by the invisible net of attraction.

'Strange how bodies can so easily ignore the dictates of the mind,' he said.

The words were a cool echo of her own turgid thoughts but she knew that she had to deny them.

'Your body troubling you?' she asked calmly, stepping into the lift and turning towards him, a look of bland enquiry plastered across her face.

'Considerably!' he said gravely, his dark eyes looking directly into hers, holding her attention as he edged closer and closer to where she stood. 'And arms folded across your chest are a dead give-away of a defensive attitude,' he murmured, crowding her almost, but not quite, to touching point.

She unfolded her arms, but held his gaze defiantly.

The doors slid closed, folding them into a false intimacy that battered at her senses.

'You told me once that my body meant nothing to you once you'd stopped loving me,' she reminded him, deciding that the best defence—after folded arms—would be attack.

'Maybe I lied!' he whispered, and moved enough to brush against her—thigh against thigh, arm against arm—sensation burning through the filmy material of her bright dress, through the rough slubbed cotton of his shirt.

Her senses shrieked in silent demand.

Lied about the attraction or about not loving me? she wondered, searching his words in an effort to ward off the invasive pressures of his body.

Opening doors saved her, and she hurried out of the lift.

'Jack's flat is two floors higher,' she said sharply when escape was denied by his following her into the fourth-floor foyer.

'But I don't have a key,' he murmured so suggestively that she shivered with a feverish panic.

'Well, you can't wait at my place!' she said nervously, crossing to her door and standing with her back to it as if to guard it against imminent invasion.

'No!' he said slowly, walking towards her until he stood only inches in front of her, looking down into her face. 'Peter might not welcome me, might he?'

His head lowered, and for a moment she thought he was going to kiss her. She held her breath, willing it to happen but at the same time deriding herself for her weakness.

'I'll just take the keys!'

He lifted Jack's car keys from her nerveless fingers, and crossed back to where the lift waited for a call from another floor.

Allysha felt her knees give way and, as the doors closed on him, she gave in to the weakness and sank to the floor, unaware that she was in the classic pose of prayer as she asked the gods to help her regain control of her life.

Nick let the lift carry him away from the fourth floor but it didn't carry him away from the torment, which accompanied him upwards with the ghost of a slight, curvaceous woman in a bright flame of a dress.

It was a fitting analogy, he decided, because in his mind Allysha and fire were forever entwined.

Not only had she engulfed his body with the searing heat of need, but her mercurial progress through life had had the flickering inconstancy of flames—enthusiasms flaring and dying as she had sought, with a manic desperation, to fill every moment with what she and her friends had termed 'fun'.

He had tried to catch that flame, to capture it, to warm himself beside it and hold it for ever in his hands—and had been badly burned for his troubles.

He sighed and stepped from the lift, forcing his mind to think about the patients they had flown back to town—to think about anything rather than Allysha.

She was awake, but still wandering sleepily around the flat, when the doorbell pealed at eleven the next morning.

Opening the door, she found Peter standing in the foyer. With a carton of milk in one hand, a packet of what looked like Danish pastries in the other, and the Sunday papers tucked under his arm he looked as if he was returning from a quick, domestic errand.

'I prefer milk to coffee, so I brought my own in case you didn't have any,' he said, as if that would explain his presence on her doorstep.

'But. . .'

'I thought I should call in and see how you got on

last night,' he added, ushering her into the flat and closing the door. 'Great view!'

She nodded, bemused by his presence. The water, ruffled by a light northerly breeze, danced and sparkled beyond her windows.

'I also thought you might like someone to talk to and, being a newly appointed friend, came to offer my services.'

Allysha smiled and nodded again, silently admitting that she was pleased to have company—although she wasn't certain there'd be much 'talking'.

'I'll put on coffee for myself,' she said, leading him through into the kitchen and reaching for a glass for his milk. 'We had an extremely late night—or early morning—and I haven't had my morning dose of caffeine! We did a double evac, with a trip to Herd Island after Castleford.'

'Yes, Jack told me,' Peter replied. 'I met him and the new chap downstairs. They were going out for breakfast but, after the way that Nick fellow frowned at me, I didn't feel tempted to ask them to join us.'

'They—he—they must have thought. . .'

The words sputtered to a halt.

'Exactly!' Peter agreed, grinning with pleasure. 'Now, won't that further our little deception without a word of a lie being spoken?'

Allysha smiled at his delight, but could not dispel a niggling uneasiness.

'Jack told me about the patient you brought in—the man who had an electric shock.' Had Peter changed the subject because he'd sensed her concern? She filled the electric kettle and switched it on, listening while he explained about tissue damage from the path the electric current had taken through the man's body and unexpected rib fractures from the muscular contractions in his chest.

In six months she had picked up more than a layman's knowledge of medicine, and understood most of what Peter was telling her.

'It was a better explanation for his chest pain than an infarct, from his point of view,' he finished, arranging the sticky pastries on the plate she'd handed him. 'But I doubt if I'd have thought of it at the time, especially when it was accompanied by such irregular heartbeats.'

Medical conversation over breakfast! It was like a replay of the past. In just such a way had she and Nick shared Sunday mornings—only Nick liked toast and marmalade! Again she recognised that it was the special joy of sharing that had made memorable the most ordinary moments—and made more agonising the loneliness that followed when the togetherness was lost.

She was grinding coffee-beans when the doorbell sounded again and she looked up at Peter, as if he might know who was outside.

'Shall I go?' he asked, and she nodded.

'This machine will take off if I leave it unattended,' she told him.

The grinding was finished a moment later and she spooned grounds into the plunger then filled it with boiling water, savouring the rich aroma.

'We brought our own pastries!'

It was Jack's voice, and she closed her eyes and clung onto the kitchen bench for support. Why was Nick doing this to her? In the six months she had lived in this complex she and Jack had never done more than meet occasionally in the lift, so Nick had to be the instigator of this social occasion!

There was more talk but she couldn't concentrate enough to follow the words, then Jack said, 'The coffee smells great.'

Allysha turned to find him behind her in the kitchen.

'I hope we're not intruding,' he said, waving another white paper bag towards her, 'but when I saw Peter in the building I thought it might be a good chance to talk over some changes to the clinic flights, now we've a full complement of doctors again.'

Jack spoke as if his idea had been a stroke of genius. His passion was the Service, and working for it—or thinking about it—occupied all his waking hours. The problem was that he seemed to assume all his staff members felt exactly the same way. Allysha knew he would have been shocked—and probably hurt—if she'd voiced any objections to this friendly invasion.

She handed him a plate for his contribution of pastries, and put two extra cups on the tray.

'Shall we sit on the balcony?'

Now Peter poked his head into the kitchen. She nodded feebly and then, knowing he'd looked in to see how she was reacting—and to give his silent support— she tried a small smile.

'You'll need an extra chair out there,' she told him, and added bravely, 'unless one of our visitors would prefer to sit inside!'

Jack would think she was joking but Nick, whom she had yet to see, would get the message!

She lifted the tray and walked straight through the living-room to the balcony, blinking at the brightness of the sun off the water.

'I'll need to get my sunglasses if we're sitting out here,' she said as she slid the tray onto the table. 'Help yourselves to coffee; I'll be back in a moment.'

She turned and hurried through the door, colliding solidly with a warm, male body.

'Throwing yourself back into my arms?' Nick's voice whispered in her ear, while his hands grasped her shoulders to steady her balance.

Move! she ordered her body, but the muscles refused to obey—unless it was to creep an infinitesimal fraction closer.

'My eyes hadn't adjusted from the light outside,' she muttered, then chided herself for the inanity of the comment. 'I need my sunglasses,' she explained.

It should have been the signal for him to release her, or for her to step hurriedly away, but. . .

'Then you'd better get them, Lys,' he murmured gruffly, easing his body from hers and turning her in the direction of the bedroom.

She walked away, although every footstep was an enormous effort of will. Her whole being had responded to his as iron filings responded to a magnet, and she could feel that illogical attraction plucking at her skin, and nerves, and sinews.

She closed her bedroom door behind her and leaned against it, like a fighter gathering strength for the next round. You can ask for a change of roster, she told herself, then she realised that she was no longer thinking about leaving—about running away from this new problem in her life! One up to you, my girl, she added silently, then pushed herself off the supporting door and hurried through to the bedroom.

A quick glance in the mirror revealed a suspicious sparkle in her eyes and definite colour in her normally pale cheeks. She splashed water on her face, acknowledging that she would need the protection of sunglasses for more than the bright reflection of light off the water.

'We were discussing our ongoing problem at Caltura,' Jack told her when she rejoined the men on her balcony. 'You've been out there more regularly than anyone over the last six months—what do you think?'

She glanced at Peter, who looked concerned and wary, then at Nick, his face half hidden behind his own sunglasses, and then back to Jack.

'I think they've had a rough deal,' she said, pouring herself a cup of coffee and taking it and a pastry across to the fourth chair. 'And, according to Matt, the problems aren't going to be fixed overnight. Whoever takes them on should be prepared to stay on that run for a couple of years to try to stabilise the situation.'

And that will cut out Nick, who is only here for a year! she thought, pleased at her own cleverness in diverting him off her flights.

'Caltura hasn't had a reliable health worker for more than a year and, unfortunately, during that time we had too many changes in our medical staff and people began to forget clinic appointments,' Jack explained to Nick. 'The health of the whole community has deteriorated as a result.'

He turned to Allysha again, and asked, 'What about the fellow who's taken on the health worker's duties, this Andrew Walsh? I didn't meet him when I was out there last week—he was away—but Matt spoke highly of him.'

'He's terrific!' Allysha replied. 'He's determined and forceful, yet persuasive when he needs to be. I've seen him talk an alcoholic out of having that ''one last'' drink without any fight or argument.'

'So, if we run into more staffing problems, he could hold things together?'

Allysha frowned, puzzled by Jack's persistence about this matter. Unless. . .

She looked at Nick. Had he said he couldn't stay? Had he decided he couldn't work in the same organisation as her?

'Andrew could hold things together,' she said slowly when she knew that she had to answer the question or attract attention by her silence, 'but he shouldn't have to do that. He has so many other things on his agenda— so many plans for the cattle property, and building projects, and tutoring in the old ways for the young people. He doesn't deserve to have his vision bogged down because we're not doing our job properly.'

She felt the surprised reaction from her listeners, strongest of all from Nick. Had her implied criticism of the organisation upset him?

'Well said, Allysha!' Peter's voice was warm with praise. 'I agree wholeheartedly and would gladly swap my clinics for Caltura if it would help, but I'm booked to attend that conference in the States later this year and I'm going on from there to an aero-medical course in Europe. It would mean they'd be in the hands of a locum again for those two months.'

'It's not that our locums aren't top doctors,' Jack said with a gusty sigh, 'but having them working at places like Caltura disrupts the continuity of service.'

'So put them somewhere else and put permanent staff at this Caltura place,' Nick suggested, and Allysha felt her lips twitching towards a smile. He had always driven straight to the core of problems, wanting them solved and then packed neatly away. Which is what he'd done with her, of course! The smile vanished.

'Who?' Jack said. 'You're the obvious solution, but I know you can only give us a year. A year would be better than six months, but if an onlooker like Allysha can see they need more than that. . .'

'Could you go to Caltura and I do your clinics?'

Allysha looked from Nick to Jack, then glanced at Peter to see how he had reacted.

'I do the mining camps and the islands where the fishing fleets call because it's different medicine. More physical injuries, more strains and sprains, but especially more surgery. I do a fortnightly trip to Wyrangi, the one big mining town we cover. We spend two days there and usually one full day of that is operating.'

'I don't know how it is in Broken Hill,' Peter said, breaking in to extend the explanation 'but up here the criteria for appointment of a doctor are five years' experience, plus paediatric, obstetric, emergency and anaesthetic experience. Although we all do surgery in our initial training, we don't need to take further courses in it to get into the Service.'

'Which may happen here soon,' Jack continued. 'Mainly because it's becoming a bigger and bigger part of our workload. Before the mining began in the area there was little call for anything beyond stitching up cuts, but with the number of mines and exploratory camps increasing we have two problems. One is the increase in work-related accidents, and the other is the number of men who require minor surgery but are unwilling to make the trip to town.'

Allysha relaxed back into her chair. They were so engrossed in their conversation that they had forgotten she was there. Not that she minded! It gave her the opportunity to study Nick from behind her dark glasses, and try to analyse the way she had felt for that moment in his arms.

Peter was explaining that, apart from a reluctance to

take time off work, the men didn't like leaving their camps unattended—or leaving their wives alone in isolated places to keep an eye on things. The skin between Nick's dark brows was puckered into a frown of concentration, an expression she knew so well that it hurt to see it.

'So, if they've got a hernia, or haemorrhoids, or other easy stuff, they head for Wyrangi, knowing Jack will fix them up in a day or two and they can get back to their camp. Once he started doing a bit of surgery the demands escalated.' Peter grinned at the new doctor, then added, 'Does that explain why he hasn't switched to Caltura?'

As Allysha watched, Nick's face lightened, and his lips stretched in an answering smile.

'It sure does,' he said, strengthening the American accent that lingered in his voice. 'So—ask me about my qualifications!'

Peter and Jack both turned to him.

'You're not going to tell me you've done a surgery unit?' Jack demanded.

'I have indeed!' Nick said, nodding with an exaggerated air of false modesty. 'You didn't ask about surgery when I contacted you to discuss the job, but I haven't spent all my spare time in the States in idle contemplation of my navel. In between emergency calls with the ''First Response'' group, I did a surgery unit at the local training hospital.

'I probably don't have your skills, but I'm confident I could handle most minor procedures without any problems. Add to that the fact that we're phone-linked most of the time so if I strike anything tricky you could talk me through it.'

The excitement simmered in his voice. The same

excitement she had heard when he'd first talked to her about his job! It was one of the things that had attracted her to him in the first place. For someone who spent a great deal of her time, and her inherited money, in pursuit of the thrill she and her friends labelled 'fun' the idea that someone could find it in his work had been especially seductive.

'So we could swap and you do my clinics,' Jack was saying when she switched her mind back to the present. 'I must say I'm thrilled with the idea.' He gave a slightly sheepish smile. 'I feel responsible for what has happened at Caltura, and I've been longing to get out there. I want to see things for myself and help this Andrew Walsh put some of his plans into practice.'

'So we're all sorted out,' Peter said, sitting back in his chair and smiling at Allysha.

She knew that he was sending her a silent message. And you've got Jack on your flights instead of Nick, the look said, but when she glanced at Nick and saw his frown deepen, she wondered if it had sounded as if Peter was trying to get rid of their visitors!

'Almost!' Jack said, reaching out to refill his coffee-cup and choose another calorie-loaded pastry. He sat back, bit into it and savoured the taste before he spoke again.

'We've one other slight hitch, and that's with pilots. Eddie is trying to sort it out, but we might be able to help him if we talk it through now.'

'Problems with Melissa Ward?' Peter asked, and Allysha looked from him to Jack, her heart sinking in her chest.

Melissa was the wife of Michael—the pilot who regularly flew Jack's clinic flights. Allysha knew that she was eventually pregnant after trying for five years and had been the first to congratulate Michael, whose whole being had radiated happiness. Surely there couldn't be complications this early?

Jack answered her.

'Her blood pressure is high, and she's having kidney problems. Her specialist wants her to go to bed for the last five months, but we all know how difficult that would be. Michael, naturally, wants to be home as much as possible, so Eddie and I are trying to work him into single-day clinics and extra on-call duties.'

'But wouldn't on-call duties take him away more often?' Nick protested.

Allysha shook her head, still upset by the news about Melissa.

'More often but not for longer periods of time,' she explained. 'Most evacuations take a maximum of five hours. The essence of the system is to get the person to a major hospital in the fastest possible time, so you go straight out and straight back.'

'With only the occasional diversion!' Jack reminded her.

'And do you think you can rearrange the pilot roster?' Peter asked, and Jack nodded.

'Theoretically we've all six pilots to call on,' he pointed out, 'because Eddie has offered to fly more, although it would take him away from his administrative duties, and I don't particularly like that option. Allysha!' He turned towards her. 'You've done the mining clinic flights with me a couple of times—would you be willing to take them on for the next few months?'

She shot a wry glance at Peter. So much for escaping Nick!

'But you don't like using women pilots on the mining

clinics,' Peter objected, coming to her rescue immediately. 'You've said yourself that Wyrangi is too rough
a town to have a woman hanging around during the
day while you're operating. It's OK for the nurse
because she's with you, but what's the pilot
supposed to do?'

'I've said I'd prefer not to have women pilots on the
run,' Jack argued, 'but we can't always have what we
want. There are women in the town, after all, plenty of
them—workers at the store and hotel, the men's wives
and daughters! It's not as if she'd be attacked or rav-
ished. I just don't like the atmosphere there.'

Allysha laughed at the disapproving expression on
his face.

'You old romantic, you!' she teased. 'I knew you
didn't like my taking those flights, but I never guessed
it was because you thought the behaviour of the men
might shock my sensibilities.'

Jack looked embarrassed but, beyond him, she could
see Nick stiffening and knew he was going to raise
some equally ridiculous objection to the scheme.

'I grew up on a sheep property,' she told Jack before
Nick could speak, 'and I learned every swear word the
shearers knew before I was four. I can take care of
myself in those situations.'

She spoke firmly, hoping to convince Jack that she
would be able to handle this new challenge com-
petently. Then she realised that she was talking herself
into working with Nick. Had Peter been trying to get
her out of that tangle when he'd argued with Jack?

And had she, subconsciously, wanted to fly with Nick
when she'd leapt in with her own assurances?

'If you've got three other operational pilots plus

Eddie, why roster Allysha to a place you'd rather not send a woman?' Nick asked.

'Because,' Jack said deliberately, 'after Eddie, she's the best we've got. Michael—all the others—are good. Exceptional, I should say! But Allysha has a special touch—a feel for the outback strips—that city-trained pilots never seem to achieve. Some of the mining camps are high in the mountains, and the approaches are tricky. Michael has flown the route often enough to know it well, and I won't make the decision—Eddie will—but, believe me, if I had to break someone else in to it I'd have to choose Allysha.'

Hearing herself praised made her squirm, but beneath the embarrassment was a fierce pride at having her ability praised by a man who had flown with experts.

'So are you asking Allysha if she's willing to swap?' Peter asked, bringing their attention back to the subject of rosters.

'I'm running it past her so she can think about it before Eddie suggests it,' Jack responded. 'She might have some other idea or might prefer not to do it, in which case we'll have to use one of the others and hope he develops the same degree of skill Michael has.'

'I'd be willing to do it,' Allysha heard herself say, and again she wondered if subconscious promptings had triggered the response. Or had she offered because she could feel waves of disapproval flowing from Nick? Had she leapt into the situation, reacting with her own contrariness, knowing that he didn't want her piloting his clinic runs?

CHAPTER FIVE

ROSTERED off for two days, Allysha spent the time studying maps of the northern mining region. She could visualise all the landing strips from the few trips she'd done on that particular clinic run, but now she had to learn about the weather conditions likely to prevail in the area and the idiosyncrasies of the wind in the mountainous region.

She had the navigation charts spread across her dining-table when Michael arrived.

'Eddie asked me to go over the route with you,' he explained, his cheerful smile unable to conceal the anxiety in his eyes.

'How's Melissa?' Allysha asked. She led him to a comfortable chair and sat by him, holding his hand while he poured out all his anxiety and despair.

'I can't let her see how worried I am,' he said frankly. 'She's feeling let down and disappointed with herself—which she shouldn't be, but I can't get her to believe that—so how can I burden her with my concern and make her feel worse?'

'Don't burden her with it—come over here and tell me!' Allysha suggested. 'You need someone to talk to about how you feel, and you know I won't pass it on.'

She made coffee and they drank it together, talking about the single-day runs which would be new to Michael.

'What did you do in Wyrangi for two days?' Allysha asked as they were bent over the charts a little later.

Before Michael could reply the doorbell heralded another visitor.

This is ridiculous, Allysha thought as she walked across the room. One week ago I was the local hermit, and now I have people popping in at all hours of the day and night.

She opened the door without any presentiment of doom, yet when she saw Nick standing in the foyer her heart first leapt and then sank, and her mind went into denial mode.

I'll never be able to work with him! The words beat in her brain like an unwanted snatch of song.

'I came down to talk about Wednesday's schedule,' he said, and she knew, from the hostility in his voice, that he'd glimpsed Michael beyond her and his mind had gone into overdrive, making erroneous assumptions.

'Come in!' she muttered through stiff lips. She could have added that Michael was here for the same reason, but she was not going to offer an explanation that might sound like an excuse.

She introduced the two men, Melissa's debility having kept the Wards from Saturday's welcoming party.

'The clinic run hops from mine site to mine site for the first day—Wednesday. Four touchdowns if you count Wyrangi, the final stopping-place for the day,' Michael explained, pointing to the dots which marked the mines. 'Your best wind is a north-easter and your worst a westerly or north-west blow!'

Allysha nodded. The north-westerly usually accompanied a depression, which could whip the winds to gale force and slash rain like solid sheets of water across the windshield. Great fun in an area where the high mineral content in the ground made instrument readings less reliable than usual, and mountains crowded the landing strips like onlookers at a disaster.

Nick drew closer to the table, bending over the charts to see the places he would be visiting. His body brushed against Allysha's arm and she had to fight against an urge to move a little closer as she leant forward over their proposed route. Would it be so wrong to feel his body heat once again—if only for a few stolen moments?

She knew that it would, yet couldn't take that single step away.

'Wyrangi's easy,' Michael said, and Allysha took the necessary step, knowing she couldn't possibly concentrate while the marginal contact was reminding her of too many other things. 'It's a company town now,' he explained to Nick, 'built on the site of an old port which was settled back in the early days. It's right on the gulf and provides a shipping point for the ore from the mines. The area is low and flat, with a proper runway for the commercial flights servicing it once a week.'

Nick continued to study the charts while his body bombarded hers with signals she found difficult to ignore, and she wondered if he was as aware of her as she was of him. Surely not!

'Jack's worried about how I'll fill two days in Wyrangi,' she said to Michael, repeating her question as she tried to distract herself with conversation. 'What did you do?'

Michael looked up and smiled—the first proper smile she'd seen since he arrived.

'I sat in the pub, of course!' he said, then relented when she protested that he couldn't have been drinking.

'Actually, I usually spent the mornings in my room upstairs—we stay at the pub, you know. At lunchtime it was down for a counter-lunch, then I'd stay on in the bar—drinking soda water. I loved listening to the yarns of the bush characters who've come to roost up there in Wyrangi, and watching the antics of the miners enjoying a few days' leave in town.'

Allysha knew that he would have relished it, absorbing the atmosphere and accents to use later in the writing he did in his spare time.

'Miners on leave in the town?' Nick echoed disapprovingly. 'No wonder Jack doesn't like taking women on that run.'

'Jack has no problem with Jane going—and she's a woman,' Allysha argued. 'Anyway, if a woman can't take care of herself in awkward situations she shouldn't be working in the Service.'

Michael looked at Allysha and then at Nick, obviously puzzled by the antagonism he sensed between them.

'Actually, Jane's engaged to a chap who manages the supermarket up there. She stays with him.' There was a hint of apology in his voice, as if he was sorry to be cutting down Allysha's argument.

'I'll manage,' she said firmly, disliking the intimations of the 'helpless woman' that were lurking in the conversation.

'I'm sure you will,' Michael agreed, then he stood up, saying, 'I'd best be off.'

Allysha waited for Nick to say that he also had to go. When he sank into a chair and pulled the flight book towards him, she realised that she was waiting in vain.

With her heart thumping irregularly, she accompanied Michael to the door.

'Thanks, Allysha!' he said quietly. 'It was good to talk about it.'

He bent and dropped a kiss on her cheek, then opened the door, called goodbye to Nick and left.

It couldn't be fear! she told herself, trying to soothe the rapid beating in her chest. She turned slowly and, on leaden feet, walked back to where Nick was making himself comfortable at her dining-room table.

'I'm going to speak to Jack about these trips,' he said, not looking up from the book.

She looked at him, knowing him so well that she could read the disapproval in the hard line of his shoulders and the determined tilt of his chin.

'You're being ridiculous, Nick,' she said quietly. During the long sleepless hours of the nights since he'd arrived in the Bay, she'd tried to convince herself that she'd been happy during her six months with the Service—happy without his presence in her life. Yet, beneath the reassuring platitudes she'd fed her mind and body, she knew it hadn't been a life at all. It had been an existence, made liveable by the pride and pleasure she felt in her job.

And now? She walked across to the windows and looked out over the restless, silvery water.

Was it better to be near him, knowing how he felt about her, or should she cut herself off from him again—and from the work she'd grown to love? She breathed in and turned to face him. It was time to take a stand.

'This is my job,' she said. 'One that I do because I enjoy it, no matter what interpretation you put on my being here. And, if Eddie Stone thinks I'm the best pilot for this run, I'm going to do it.'

The firm chin tilted a notch higher, and his brown eyes, now that he'd decided to look at her, flared with a yellow sheen of anger.

'You're doing it to prove something!' he snapped. 'Exactly as you used to do when you took those ridiculous irresponsible dares. You nearly broke your leg trying to work your way around the dance hall without touching the ground, if I remember rightly. And you're doing the same thing now.'

'So what if I am?' she retorted, pleased that her fear and uncertainty had turned to anger. 'It's none of your business what I do or why I do it. And if you want ridiculous, the most ridiculous dare I ever took on was—'

She stopped abruptly, aware that her unleashed tongue had almost led her into another disaster.

'Was what?' he asked, rising slowly to his feet, and stepping towards her.

She backed away, but came up against a wall.

'Was what, Allysha?' he asked again, taking another step that brought him within touching distance. 'Was it to win the staid young doctor who turned up at that particular Bachelor Ball? Was I a dare? Was the table-walking stunt and subsequent sprained ankle a way of getting my attention?'

His brown eyes burned their rage into hers, alive as glowing coals in the exaggerated stillness of his body. It was the stillness of control, she knew, the stillness of a fury held in check by the tightest of reins—not ready, yet, to be unleashed.

And all she could think of was the feel of his cool hands on her heated skin—soothing as ice on the throbbing ankle!

'I often wondered,' he continued, in a falsely conversational voice that brought her mind back to the present and notched her anxiety tighter. 'Why else would the darling of the social set suddenly become interested in

a country doctor—especially one with such unsocial
hours of duty as a Flying Doctor?'

'I didn't know how unsocial the hours were,' she
said nervously, obeying an instinct to say something—
anything—then realising, belatedly, that the words
were the verbal equivalent of petrol, flung carelessly
onto the fire of his anger.

He took the one step closer and stretched his arms
out to touch the wall on either side of her, cutting off
any chance of retreat. He didn't know that she couldn't
move anyway—that her legs had weakened to the point
of instability, and her feet felt as if they were glued to
the floor. His head bent slowly and deliberately towards
her. Mesmerised, she watched his lips and felt the ache
of longing.

'Perhaps it's time for me to issue the dare,' he whispered, lips now too close to see. She closed her eyes,
trying to blot out his presence, and tensed her body,
expecting a vengeful assault. 'How long would you
give me to get you into bed?' he murmured. 'One
month? Two?'

Her heart was beating so fast that she thought that
he must hear it and her mind was a chaotic jumble of
despair and anger, with silly threads of hope entangling
things even more.

'Or a week, maybe?' he added, close enough for her
to feel the words brush her skin.

Rigid against the wall, she waited for his kiss but,
when it came, it wasn't fierce, or angry, or vengeful.

Instead, it eased across her lips, soft as the skim of
butterfly wings, and a tiny cry of need, or want, or
disappointment, fluttered from her heart.

'I think a week should be enough,' he added hate-
fully, and Allysha tried to pull herself together—to

resist the physical spell he was casting while his lips derided her and his thoughts denounced her.

'Please, Nick?' she muttered, opening her eyes to add their pleas to her words.

But his face blurred out of focus and he must have taken the request the wrong way for his mouth closed on hers again, not gentle this time but as hard and demanding as she'd expected earlier.

Her body responded with the fierce hunger generated by the year apart—a year of yearning need and cold loneliness. Her lips parted beneath his, eager to taste him, to feel his mastery and answer his desire. Their bodies remembered things their minds had never thought of, fitting to each other as if especially moulded to each other's shape.

As the kiss deepened into another phase of sensuality that was the preliminary to sexual fulfilment he dropped his hands from the wall, and put his arms around her to draw her hard against his body.

In some dim corner of her mind she remembered his words and sadness bit into the physical delight, not killing it but, instead, adding a piquancy she knew should shame her.

She didn't know she was crying until he lifted his head from hers for a moment and straightened up, letting her nerveless body drop back against the wall when he flung away from her, swearing under his breath.

'You see what you've done to me?' he yelled, spinning back to face her and flinging his arms wide. 'You've made me into some kind of animal! Hell! I was even playing your games! Flirting with your stupid dares! And stop crying!'

The last infuriated order made her lift a trembling hand to her cheek. She wiped at the moisture and then looked at her damp fingers, too shocked by what had happened to know how to react—let alone respond! Crying? She *never* cried.

'I think you'd better go,' she quavered when he'd stormed around her dining-table a few times.

He looked at her and frowned, as if surprised that she'd finally spoken.

'Of course!' he said, stopping his speedy perambulations around her room. But when he made no move towards the door she pushed her body away from the wall and walked across to open it.

He followed her, the emotion that raged within him flaring like electricity from his body and burning a pathway down her back. She stood aside to let him past and he walked through to the foyer then turned, frowned at her again and said, 'Are you all right?' in a harsh, demanding voice.

'Of course!' she told him coldly, pleased to find some sanity had returned. He kissed you for a dare, she reminded herself, and felt pride stiffen her weakened muscles.

'Well, good for you!' he growled and turned away to summon the lift.

She closed the door, unable to bear the sight of his rigid back and sternly disapproving shoulders.

It should be a great year! she told herself glumly, then she lifted her hand and brushed her fingers across lips that still tingled from his touch. Could such a strong physical reaction to each other exist without love? she wondered. Or with a one-sided love?

She stared out through her windows, her eyes taking in the beauty of the scene but her mind following thoughts far removed from nature's wondrous display.

The love she felt for Nick had not diminished over

the past twelve months. It might have been tarnished by his harsh words when they parted, and it might have been buried under the mountains of study and work she'd done, but it still existed, like the bright shining light of a candle behind neglected, smoke-blackened glass.

For all the good that would do her!

She sighed and returned to the charts. In nine hours and twenty-five minutes she would be out at the airport, ready for a five-thirty departure, and, if she wanted to prove she was as good a pilot as her superiors thought her, she'd better put all thoughts of Nick Furlong out of her mind. After all, she'd had enough practice at that over the past year.

But he wasn't with you in the flesh, her heart reminded her head, and she sighed again.

Nick rode up the two levels to Jack's flat then pressed the down button and rode back to the ground floor, deciding he had to tell the manager that he wouldn't take the apartment that would become vacant next week. It would be bad enough having to see Allysha during working hours but he realised now that he couldn't handle living this close to her.

He'd gone down to see her, at Jack's suggestion, to arrange a lift out to the airport with her in the morning, but had forgotten everything when confronted by a man in her flat. Another man! Was she playing Peter for a fool? That had been his first thought—and an unworthy one, he knew. But knowing only made him feel sick because, deep down, he was aware that it was his own jealousy, not any regard for Peter's feelings, that had caused his annoyance.

The pager on his belt interrupted his pointless mental recriminations, and he hurried to the phone in the foyer to call in to the answering service.

'Jack's on his way to the airport for an evac flight and the radio alarm's gone off. Katie's on her way to the Base; could you get over there in case it's something that can be handled as a consultation? If it's an emergency that needs a doctor, Jack might be able to divert. He's on a Priority Two—child with a broken leg on a cattle property.'

'I'll go straight to the Base,' he promised, and walked outside to flag down one of the taxis that cruised the Esplanade.

'Didn't think you used the Base much at night,' the taxi driver remarked. 'Thought you'd gone all modern with phones and answering services and such.'

'We have, to a great extent,' Nick explained, 'but some families are out of cellular phone range and have to rely on radio. The radio alarm signal travels by phone cable to the answering service in the same way the School of Distance Education lessons travel from our radio receivers at the Base to their school building.'

'But the answering service can't do the doctoring, eh? They still need to call you chaps in sometimes!'

Nick agreed. In his early days in Broken Hill most of the communications had been by radio and the Base had been staffed by radio officers twenty-four hours a day. Using an after-hours answering service reduced staff and freed money to go towards the cost of increased aircraft operational hours.

'Here you are! Hope it's not serious,' the cabby said, pulling up into the parking area at the back of the building.

'I hope not, too,' Nick agreed, knowing that the last thing he needed before his first clinic flight was an all-night emergency.

'Hi, Nick.' Katie greeted him with a smile, and waved her hand to a pot of coffee and cup. 'I've spoken to the woman who radioed the alarm. She lives on the eastern side of the cape—do you know about those people?'

'The ones Jack calls the "fringe dwellers"?'

Katie nodded.

'This woman, Skye, lives with her three children and another family on the beach about six kilometres from the road north. It seems all the children had walked along the beach early in the afternoon, and half an hour ago one of them came running back to get help. Apparently they trapped a stingray in the shallows and were trying to catch it when one of the younger boys stood on it. The tail whipped around and caught his leg.

'The older children began to carry him home and sent a youngster on ahead. Skye radioed to alert us, and will call again when the rescue party arrive back at the camp.'

Stingrays! Nick thought, shaking his head while he tried to remember. He'd read up on marine stingers, sea snakes and other venomous creatures when he'd applied for the twelve-month posting at Rainbow Bay. Sea creatures with spikes—there was something unusual in the treatment!

He was walking towards the bookshelves when he remembered, but he pulled out the marine toxins book to make sure.

'Can you radio Skye?' he asked Katie, and saw her turn immediately to the radio controls.

'This is Dr Nick Furlong, Skye. He wants to talk to you.' She waved her hand towards the microphone propped above the transmitter. 'Just talk,' she said to Nick.

'Skye, you will need hot water—could you put some on to boil immediately?'

'Hot water?' came the bemused echo.

'If it was a stingray hot water will ease the pain almost instantaneously,' he explained. 'You will have to be careful not to burn the skin but make it as hot as the child can bear. Clean the wound first, then keep it immersed in the hot water, adding more as it cools, for at least half an hour or until it's no longer hurting. You go and put the water on and call back once the child is with you to tell me how he's feeling.

'How primitive are the conditions there?' he asked Katie. 'Will she have to light a fire?'

Katie smiled.

'I think they'd have gas,' she said, 'but it was a good idea to let her know. Even with gas it will take a while to get water hot enough.'

She reached across and poured herself another cup of coffee from the insulated pot. Her movements were delicately graceful, and he noticed that her hands were slim and shapely. He'd been getting to know the staff during his first two days at the Base—a surface impression of busy, dedicated people. Yet he sensed a diffidence in Katie, as if the swinging curtain of long, mousy hair hid uncertainty or insecurity as well as a face he thought would be attractive if it was seen more clearly more often.

'Do you mind these night calls?' he asked, and was surprised when her head lifted and the hair fell back, revealing a strongly boned face and wide-spaced hazel eyes that shone with commitment.

'I love them,' she said and then shrugged, embarrassed by her enthusiasm. 'I think I should have been born a generation or two earlier,' she admitted ruefully, 'back when radio was the main link between the people in the outback. To me it has a special magic—invisible waves of sound beaming out through the air, linking people who might never see another human being.'

'Phones aren't the same?' he queried, and again she shrugged, but this time the curtain of hair swung forward and he knew that he'd lost the tenuous contact he'd made with her.

'Phones work with technology, and computerised parts, and satellites,' she pointed out. 'To me, it's not the same as sending a message out into the air five hundred miles away and having it picked up here. I know they used advanced application of the same theories but, to me, there's no magic in a phone.'

Nick would have liked to ask her where the magic was these days, knowing he'd lost touch with it a year ago, but the radio called to them and he knew that it would have been a stupid question anyway.

'The kids are back. Clayton's been vomiting and he's very pale and sweaty; he has cramps and you can hear him screaming.'

'Have you tried the hot water?' Nick asked.

'It's not hot yet,' the woman wailed, and he imagined he could feel her frustration. Was Katie right about the power of radio?

'Wrap a blanket around the child. The severity of the pain will induce shock. Now, tell me about the wound. Have the spines penetrated the skin?' He was anxious to verify that the injury had come from a sting-ray, not something more lethal.

'There's a red mark up his leg about four inches long. There are a few bleeding holes at the top of the mark, just below his knee.'

Nick visualised the child's leg.

'The serrated stinger is at the base of the tail. Part
of the redness could be from the whip of the tail, and
the wounds are from the stinger,' he explained. 'Wash
the wound now, and use some of the water you're
boiling to wet a sponge or piece of cloth. Press it against
the open wounds or pour a little of the water over them.'

He paused, wanting the listeners to absorb the information before he gave the next instructions.

'When the water is hot enough put it into a container
of some kind. If you have a child's plastic bath he
could kneel in it to immerse the injured part of his leg.
Remember hot, but not scalding, water and keep adding
a little more to keep it as hot as he can bear.'

Again he paused, flicking through the little book to
see if it offered more advice.

'The water's ready now and my friends are fixing a
bath.' Skye sounded less strained.

'Good. Now, while they're doing that, did you get a
blanket? Is he warm?'

'I've wrapped a shawl around him, and given him a
drink,' Skye explained.

'That's good,' Nick assured her. 'Give him plenty to
drink now and later. Do you have a medical chest? It
would be wise to give him an antihistamine in case he
suffers an allergic reaction.'

As he asked the question he was aware of Katie
stirring by his side, and looked across to see her shake
her head.

'We only use natural remedies,' Skye informed him,
and he put a hand over the microphone to hide the sigh
that escaped his lips. He was all for natural remedies
in cases where the body's own defence system could
handle an illness or infection, but to deny children

access to drugs that could save their lives was, to him, dangerous.

'Then something to relieve the pain might be appropriate,' he suggested, 'and keep an eye on him. If he reacts to the toxins his breathing will be affected, and you should get him to medical help as soon as possible.'

There was silence from the radio for a few moments, then a man spoke.

'We've got the boy's leg in the water,' he said, 'and he says it's not hurting as much.'

'Heat kills the toxins,' Nick explained. 'Keep it there until he tells you it's better. How's his colour? And the cramps?'

'He seems OK,' the man said, 'but we'll put him in the truck as soon as we can and drive towards town. There's a CB radio in the old bomb; we can call for help if anything happens. Once we're at Walgar the ambulance could reach us.'

'I suppose that's the best I can hope for,' Nick said to Katie, then switched on to talk again.

'I'll stay here at the Base until you're ready to leave. Contact us before you set out, and let me know how the boy is.'

He signed off.

'Those people do care about their children,' Katie told him. 'I've been up there and met a lot of them because they are the bulk of our radio users.'

Nick smiled at her earnest championship of the 'fringe dwellers'.

'And why's that?' he asked. 'Are phones too "civilised" for them?'

Katie laughed.

'I suppose they might be,' she said. 'But the main reason they have the radios is because the children have their lessons by radio through the School of Distance Education. Lucky kids! School under the coconut palms at the edge of the beach!'

'Maybe not so lucky if they suffer because of their parents' beliefs,' Nick reminded her. 'Although I've seen people whose systems have reacted to the overload of all the drugs and chemicals that abound in our so-called civilised world. I suppose you can't blame these families for trying to return to a simpler, cleaner, purer lifestyle. The fact that they're going to put the little fellow in the car and head towards medical help—just in case—makes me feel better about their values.'

Katie smiled, and sipped at her coffee.

'You could go home,' he suggested. 'I'll wait for the call and lock up.'

'And let you turn off my precious radio!' she mocked, and again he glimpsed a lively young woman behind the sheltering hair. 'No way! I'm staying right here. Will the child be all right? Is a reaction likely?'

'I don't know,' he admitted. 'Allergic reactions can occur immediately, but every person is affected differently. I heard a story once about an old aboriginal who walked into one of the small community hospitals with a brown snake on the end of his spear.'

Katie's eyes sparkled with interest, encouraging him to continue.

' ''This fella bit me,'' he said, brandishing the spear at the recoiling sister.

' ''Where did it bite you?'' the sister asked, recognising the reptile as deadly.

' ''Out by Five Mile Bore,'' he said.

'Of course, it wasn't quite the information she wanted but it caused further heart flutters in the nurse because the bore was every bit of five miles away, and if he'd walked that far the poison was well and truly spread through his system.'

'Did she look for a wound?' Katie asked. 'Had he been bitten?'

'There were what looked like fang marks on his ankle,' Nick replied, 'but when he told her it had happened at daybreak, nothing added up. Anyway, she put him to bed in the hospital, started IV fluids and radioed the Flying Doctor Base. They advised continuing the fluids, and to have antivenin and antihistamine drawn up ready to administer with the fluid in case he showed some reaction.'

'And he recovered without either?'

Katie's smile lit up her face, confirming his belief that an attractive woman was hiding behind her shyness.

'No!' Nick told her. 'Five hours later he began shivering and shaking. The reaction had set in with a vengeance. The sister radioed for an evacuation and began administering the antivenin very slowly. A plane picked him up an hour later and took him back to town, where he recovered nicely.'

'So, you're not convinced Skye's little boy won't react at some stage?' she said, the shy smile lingering on her face.

'Would you be?' he parried, standing up to return the book to the bookshelves.

The call that the party was setting out for town came soon afterwards and Katie shut down the radio, let the answering service know they were going and, together, they left the building.

'How did you get here?' Katie asked, looking around for a second car in the car park.

'Taxi,' Nick explained. 'I'm picking up a new car on Saturday but, until then, I'm dependent on cabs.'

'I'll run you home,' she offered. 'Are you still staying with Jack?'

'For the time being,' he said, his mind returning to the thought of alternative accommodation and thence to Allysha.

They drove in silence, Nick too preoccupied with his own unsatisfactory thoughts to force a conversation with someone he knew was exceptionally quiet. Then, as Katie turned the car into the curving drive of The Bay Towers, they saw Peter emerge from the front doors and walk jauntily off in the opposite direction.

Nick's small growl was matched by a despairing sigh from Katie as she braked suddenly, then stopped to let him out.

'I'll see you next week. Enjoy your trip up north,' she said, but the laughter had gone from her voice and the smile she tried was strained.

He was momentarily distracted by her reversion to the shy girl he'd first met, then he saw Peter's back disappear around the corner of the drive and he forgot Katie and whatever was bothering her as he battled to control a surging, violent jealousy.

CHAPTER SIX

IT WAS still dark when Allysha arrived at the airport next morning and she turned on lights and opened the hangar, then hooked the towing dolly to the plane. Jeff would be here shortly, but keeping busy meant that she didn't have to think about Nick.

Once the plane was on the tarmac she returned to the pilots' tiny office and phoned the control tower for the latest weather report, then faxed through her flight plan. Voices in the hangar told her that the crew had arrived but she stayed in the office, knowing that Jeff would have the cabin door open. They could load their gear without her for once.

'All set, and your passengers are on board.' Jeff's head appeared around the office doorframe as he relayed his message.

'Passengers?' she queried.

'Lady with two babies.'

'Two babies?' Allysha repeated weakly, then she remembered Carol Benson, the wife of a miner she had met at Aunt Steph's house some months ago. She'd been expecting twins.

She hurried out to the plane, nodding to Nick and Jane who were discussing what to take in front of the open stock cabinets.

'Hope you don't mind taking me home.' Carol's voice greeted her as she climbed into the cabin.

'But I thought you were closer to Wooli,' Allysha said, peering into the baby capsules Jeff had strapped on top of the stretcher. The two tiny mites were sleeping soundly, held securely in their beds by wide Velcro straps. 'Aren't they beautiful?' she breathed, turning to Carol with all the wonder she felt shining in her eyes.

Carol smiled and nodded, then added the predictable, 'When they're asleep! I was going to fly back to Wooli and have Bill pick me up there,' she explained, 'but when the twins were born he went into a panic. Reckoned they were too small to take back to an isolated place like our mine, so he got a job at Twin Mountain. He drove out there last week, but Jack suggested I fly. It's your second stop, so you'll have a chance to hear them in action before we get there.'

Allysha smiled, but something in Carol's story intrigued her enough to ask, 'How big did he expect them to be? Large baby size, or something like a three-year-old?'

Carol's laughter rang out.

'I asked him that myself, but he just shook his head and looked bewildered.'

Leaning over the closer capsule, Allysha ran her finger very gently over the soft downy head, her body filled with a sadness she couldn't define.

'OK! We're ready.'

Jane's voice distracted her and she turned to see the flight nurse securing the equipment bags. Nick stood in the doorway, an unreadable expression on his face.

Recalling how they'd parted last night, Allysha murmured an incoherent remark to Carol and hurried to the cockpit. Then she remembered the door, which she considered her personal responsibility, and came back to lock it after Jeff had pushed it closed.

'You sit up front with Allysha,' Jane was saying to Nick. 'That way, Carol and I can talk babies without any masculine interruptions or contempt.'

'I like babies,' he protested, bending in turn to examine each tiny form. Allysha fastened the door and walked past him, back to the controls.

'You can still sit up front and see the country,' Jane insisted and, as the plane began to move towards the runway, he dropped into the co-pilot's seat.

She was busy enough with take-off procedures to ignore him, Allysha decided, but ignoring the physical responses of her body was much harder. You can do this, she told herself, forcing her mind beyond her body's promptings and concentrating on the mechanics of the job.

Once in the air, her tension eased. The dawn take-off brought them up to meet the sun, a fiery golden ball rising out of the dark waters of the sea and lighting them in turn to a palette of colours—azure, jade, aquamarine and turquoise—colours as varied as the depth and the spreading shelves of coral reef hidden beneath them.

'No wonder you love flying,' Nick murmured, and she turned to him, the beauty of the sunrise blotting out all other thought. His eyes looked into hers and she thought she saw the tenderness of love, but when she blinked and looked again there was only sadness.

'We fly over the first range, then turn north and follow its line. The first camp is on a spur that leads off to the west. On a cloudless day like today you'll see the cleared strip from a fair way out; watch for the steel tower that's part of the mine rigging.'

I sound like a tourist guide, she thought, then stiffened her shoulders. That was the part she had to play—the dedicated professional—the best person for what could sometimes be a difficult job.

Nick saw the tiny movement because he was alert to every nuance in her voice, every quiver of her body. He clasped his hands firmly in his lap to stop them reaching out to touch her, and peered through the window.

He saw the clearing and the tower, but only minutes before Allysha brought the plane smoothly down onto the strip. Jane had the door open to provide steps for them by the time he reached the cabin.

'The mine manager picks us up,' she told him, handing him an equipment bag to carry. 'They've a room in the recreation block set up as a surgery, and good equipment supplied by the mine. The safety officers at all the camps have passed advanced first-aid exams. They can cope with most minor accidents and they arrange our appointments and do follow-up work for us.'

Nick said, 'See you soon,' to Carol, who was lifting a fretful baby out of its capsule, and followed Jane out of the plane, feeling uncomfortable that he hadn't said goodbye to Allysha.

But personal thoughts were soon forgotten. The first patient had an inflamed hand, and was obviously in severe pain. Nick examined it, probing at the inflammation that extended down the index finger.

'Is your finger sore?' he asked, puzzled by the blanched appearance of the fingertip.

'The top of it is numb,' he said. 'It's the rest of my hand that hurts. Do you think I've been bitten by a spider or scorpion?'

Nick searched the reddened skin but, apart from a black mark scarcely bigger than a pin-prick on the tip of the affected finger, there was no sign of a bite.

'When did it first feel sore?' he asked, prodding at

the whitened tip and frowning as he tried to find a logical explanation.

'Started throbbing a couple of days ago,' his patient said, with the laconic casualness of a man too busy to take much notice of minor injuries.

'And what had you been doing before that?'

The man thought for a moment.

'It was the day after I greased the pump machinery,' he said, nodding with satisfaction that he'd pinned down a particular day in his busy life. 'I remember because I'd caught the tip of that finger with the grease-gun and I wondered if that's what had made it sore. But a little prick like that wouldn't swell up my whole hand. It didn't even fester.'

Nick smiled at him, and prodded the tip of the finger again.

'Just jabbed it, did you?' he asked. 'Or could you have injected grease into it when you punctured the skin?'

The man lifted his hand and peered at the suspect finger.

'I reckon some could have gone in,' he said. 'It's an electric gun—got great pressure.'

'Enough to shoot a considerable amount of grease through your skin, by the feel of things,' Nick told him, taking hold of the hand again. 'In the early stages you might have noticed a bit of grease oozing out of the hole, but once it closed the trouble was hidden.'

'So what will you do?' the man asked, peering at his finger as if unable to believe that an injection of grease might have caused so much trouble.

'Open it up and clean it out,' Nick said. 'I'll give you a local anaesthetic, cut down there—' he indicated the flashy pad '—and sew it up afterwards.'

He stood up and spoke to Jane, who produced a scalpel and suture pack while he drew up Marcaine for a digital block.

The grease was packed against soft tissue and he had to squeeze as much as possible out before scraping at the remnants, anxious to avoid any nerve or blood vessel damage.

The swelling and pain in the rest of the man's hand indicated that infection was present, and he took a swab for culturing. That couldn't be done until later, but he would be able to order a different antibiotic if the culture showed an unpredictable microbial mix. After some scraping and cleaning, he examined it once again through a magnifying lens. He flushed the wound with alcohol, silently debating whether he should leave it open for topical antibiotic treatment to decrease the risk of an infection that could lead to gangrene.

'Would you take a few days off work and report to the safety officer for a new dressing each day?' he asked the man, although he suspected what the answer would be.

'For a little cut like this?' His patient laughed. 'The blokes would call me a sissy. Anyway, we're a day behind on production because we had to stop work the day I greased the pumps, and if we don't catch up we can't take leave.'

'Won't, not can't,' Jane pointed out, peering over Nick's shoulder to examine the wound. 'The men are all paid bonuses, depending on production. It isn't the boss standing over them with a big stick that stops them taking leave—it's their own determination to have as much money as possible to spend while they're away.'

The man grinned, and shrugged. 'Got to make the most of our days off, haven't we?' he said.

Nick shook his head.

'Well, I don't know about that but, if you're going to be working, I'll sew it up. I'll give you a course of antibiotics, and if the swelling hasn't gone down in three days you contact me immediately. You're likely to lose that finger-tip if we can't stop the infection.'

He stitched the finger neatly, and bound it up.

'Would they have a leather finger-guard here?' he asked Jane, and waited while she went through the supplies in the clinic cabinet.

'More of them than anything else. They must expect the men to keep working.'

She handed him a leather guard and he fitted it over the bandage, gave the man a course of antibiotics and watched him head straight back to work.

'Your next patient's not as easy,' Jane warned him. 'He burnt his leg when he walked too close to a steam duct that was venting about six weeks ago, and Jack's been trying to persuade him ever since that it needs a graft.'

The man was shown in by the safety officer, and Jane knelt to remove the dressings.

'I'm Frank Wells,' the man said, holding out his hand as he introduced himself. 'The other doc's been trying everything on this leg, but it doesn't seem to be getting better.'

Frank hitched himself onto the examination couch and Jane removed the dressings, while Nick checked the man's file. Jack hadn't seen the wound until three days after the burn occurred. The safety officer had treated it and dressed it, but Jack had found it badly infected. He had first used the enzymatic Travase to remove necrotic debris, hoping to save all the viable tissue, but the wound—which had begun as a burn the size of a man's palm—was not significantly reduced. He had switched to silver sulphadiazine ointment, and begun treating the wound as a tropical ulcer.

'Well, it's too deep for a skin graft now,' Nick said bluntly. 'Closing a superating wound like that would be a recipe for disaster.'

He looked his patient in the eye and continued. 'Now, unless you want to lose your leg, you've got to forget about work and rest it.'

As Frank opened his mouth to argue Nick held up his hand.

'Don't bother telling me about work schedules or production goals,' he said firmly, 'because I'm not interested. If that wound deepens it will affect the integrity of the bone, and you will lose your leg—so what's it to be?'

Frank turned pale and his jaw moved, as if he was literally chewing on Nick's unpalatable words.

'I'll take a few days off,' he mumbled.

'A few days is not enough,' Nick continued remorselessly. 'You'll need a week minimum. And you'll need to come up to Wyrangi with us, where the sister at the hospital can keep an eye on you and change the dressing.'

'Well, that's not a bad idea,' Frank drawled, his demeanour changing perceptibly enough to make Nick immediately suspicious.

'You won't be coming up to Wyrangi to go on a binge,' he warned. 'You'll be on double-strength antibiotics that will make you feel sick when you're lying around doing nothing, and would half kill you if you take them with alcohol.'

'You don't have to threaten me with your pills,' Frank said, looking remarkably cheerful. 'I stopped drinking years ago, but I've a girlfriend works at the pub. I reckon a little bit of a cuddle while I'm resting won't hurt my leg none!'

It was Nick's turn to smile.

'I reckon it won't!' he agreed, pulling on a clean glove in order to spread Silvazine thickly onto the wound.

He left Jane to dress it, and stepped outside to speak to the safety officer. He would be responsible for seeing that the first patient continued on antibiotics, and for arranging sick leave for Frank.

'Grab a cup of coffee from the machine while Frank packs his bag,' Jane suggested when the formalities were concluded and the safety officer had driven off with Frank. 'Who knows when we'll have time to stop again?'

'What about Allysha and our passenger?' he asked. 'Don't they get coffee?'

He was used to running clinics on farming properties, where the pilot was always welcomed as part of the medical crew and plied with refreshment while the doctor and nurse worked.

'All the pilots carry a Thermos and snacks—particularly on this run, where they like to stay near the plane at the smaller camps. We had a fellow ran amok a year or so ago. Went troppo, as they say, and thought he'd fly home to see his mum. Fortunately Eddie was the pilot and, as the man released the brakes and the plane rolled forward, Eddie calmly drove the mine manager's new four-wheel-drive out onto the airstrip in front of it. He decided it was better to buckle the undercarriage than lose the plane.'

'And a man's life,' Nick added, and saw Jane smile.

'I doubt he considered the man's life for a moment,'

she said. 'Any more than he considered possible damage to the four-wheel-drive, although the mine manager
was practically in tears as he watched the proceedings.
All Eddie cared about was saving his precious plane.'

'And did he?' Nick asked.

'With only a dent!' Jane responded. 'Apparently the
engine stalled when the underneath of the fuselage hit
the vehicle and the fellow got out to yell at Eddie and
they grabbed him. By that time Jack was on the scene
and he sedated him so they could transport him back
to the Bay for treatment.'

Nick smiled, but the underlying uneasiness he had
been feeling since he had found Allysha working in
the Flying Doctor Service grew stronger. He could tell
himself that it was none of his business, reassure himself with his own knowledge of her ability and Eddie's
assessment that she was the best, but he couldn't dispel
the fear that churned so relentlessly in his stomach.

Their transport pulled up outside the building, and
he lifted the equipment bag and followed Jane out. They
drove through neat rows of cabins, then a short distance
along a cleared but rough road towards the airstrip.

Allysha and Carol were standing in the shade cast
by the plane; both were swaying lightly and as they
drew closer he could see that they each held a baby.

'Another passenger for you,' Jane called to Allysha
and she looked up and blinked at them, as if she'd been
so lost in her contemplation of the infant that she'd
been startled by their arrival.

He saw a faint wash of colour rise in her cheeks and
half smiled, remembering how she would deny that
she blushed. As she climbed back into the plane other
memories returned—memories of the wild, madcap girl
who laughed and flirted and ran with a fast, much older

crowd, yet who'd been, he discovered, emotionally reserved and inexperienced beneath her brash exterior.

Heat burned in his body as images flashed in his mind.

Fine time to start thinking about sex! he berated himself, following Frank and the women into the cabin. But as he watched Allysha lower the baby into its capsule and saw the little smile that hovered on her lips as she murmured to the baby he felt a pain that wasn't physical need or sexual hunger.

'You sit up front, Frank,' he said so peremptorily that it must have sounded like an order because Allysha straightened in surprise and Frank made his way forward without protest.

He sank into the seat behind Jane, fastened the seat belt and closed his eyes. He'd found it hard to understand, in the early days of their relationship, what the beautiful, vibrant, fun-loving young woman she'd been could see in a dull, work-obsessed doctor like himself. Found it hard to believe that she could love him as she said she did.

Which had made it easier for him to convince himself that she didn't really love him—that he was a diversion like the other games she played—and to tell himself that he didn't care much either.

'Twin Mountain is a bigger camp.' Jane turned in her seat to speak to him and he looked out the cabin window, surprised to find that they had finished climbing and had levelled out over the mountain range again. 'I do a women's clinic for the wives and female staff. You have a diabetic we check each fortnight—he's pretty good with his own testing and self-regulation, and has been on a diet.'

'Been on a diet in a mining camp where all meals

are provided in a camp kitchen?' Nick asked, pleased to have something to divert his mind from thoughts of the past.

Jane stood up from her seat, smiled and took a little bow.

'On a diet out here,' she confirmed, 'and all thanks to yours truly!'

'Tell me about it,' he suggested, seeing the pride she felt in her achievement.

'Well, they drink a bit after their shifts and there's no point in trying to stop that but, although they work physically hard, the majority of them were overweight.'

'So what can you do in a situation like this?'

'Start in the community kitchen,' she said. 'I worked out the number of kilojoules in their beer consumption—they're on a set ration during work periods—and did a rough estimate of the kilojoules an average-sized miner would work off each day. Then I tackled the cook, and together we decided on menus that, with the beer, would be enough to maintain the weight of your average healthy male but begin reducing the weight in the tubby ones.'

'You tried to cut down on these fellows' food and didn't get lynched?' Nick asked, amazed at Jane's temerity.

'They didn't realise it had happened,' Jane assured them. 'They like their stews and casseroles, so all we had to do was reduce the meat and add more vegetables. Same thing with pasta dishes—less meat, more vegetables in the sauces. I was lucky because the cook was agreeable from the beginning, and then became the prime mover. He swears he now makes meatballs with absolutely no meat in them, and no one knows!'

Nick chuckled and, as the plane began its descent,

he found himself looking forward to his visit to Twin Mountain—if only to see the results of Jane's subversive 'diet'.

Allysha stayed in the cockpit until everyone had left the plane, fiddling unnecessarily with the controls. Holding the baby had brought an ache of emptiness to her arms and her heart, and she wondered how different things might have been if Nick's preoccupation with work hadn't fired her old rebellious spirit and made her accept the invitation to the Milgrove B and S Ball— the most talked-about of all the infamous Bachelor and Spinster revels.

'Frank says he'll stay with the plane. Come up to the canteen and sample the cook's low-calorie cake,' Jane called, and she pushed herself reluctantly out of the seat.

Two off-road vehicles were parked by the plane. Bill Benson was fastening the baby capsules into the back seat of one, while Carol supervised. Allysha could feel their pride and protective devotion from where she stood. It was like a living, palpable force—a uniting bond as strong as love itself.

'Come on,' Jane urged. 'Say goodbye to Carol and the babies, and climb aboard.'

She obeyed the command, wishing Carol luck and promising to have morning tea with her on the next clinic flight. Turning back to the other vehicle, she found Jane settled comfortably into the front seat and climbed reluctantly into the rear.

As they bounced over the rutted road that led to the main camp she held onto the seat with both hands, trying to keep her body away from Nick's—to prevent the contact she knew would fire her senses with longing, and fill her heart with pain.

'Are there other children at the camp?' Nick asked, and Jane turned to answer him.

He can't be feeling what I feel, Allysha realised sadly. So yesterday's kiss was exactly what he said it was—a challenge, not an intimation that some of the passion he'd felt for her remained as desire, or even lust!

She tried to listen to the conversation, taking in the fact that there were three families and, with the Benson twins, a total of seven children under five. But her mind had strayed too far back into the past for her to concentrate and she was pleased when they pulled up outside the main building and Jane led Nick to the surgery, while the manager suggested that he accompany her to the canteen.

Nick watched her walk away, his own confusion heightened by a sadness he had sensed in her.

'This way,' Jane said, and he followed her into the building, through a room where a group of men and women waited, into a well-equipped surgery.

'X-ray?' he said, staring in amazement at the machine he could see through a glass wall that separated the surgery from a smaller room.

'The mine owners provided it,' Jane explained. 'When they were setting up the Twin Mountain camp they asked Jack what was needed. He explained that simple fractures, if correctly diagnosed, could be set here, saving injured men a trip to Wyrangi with us and the unnecessary expense of getting back on company flights.'

Nick nodded. It made sense to have the facility. Particularly when he'd heard that there were two smaller camps within easy helicopter reach of Twin Mountain.

'And who operates it?' he asked, and Jane grinned at him.

'You doctors are supposed to know how they work,' she told him, 'but, in case you've forgotten, there's a manual.'

She must have seen his doubt reflected on his face, for she relented and added, 'It's a simple, fool-proof machine and both I and the local safety officer, a woman called Belle Stephens, spent a day with the technician when it was installed. We can both take pictures if you need them.'

Much relieved, he sent her off to do her clinic and called in his first patient. White patches on the man's skin were symptomatic of pityriasis versicolor, a fungal infection of the skin that he knew was more common in the tropics than in the hot but arid areas he was used to around Broken Hill.

'I know it's only a fungus, and it doesn't hurt. I'm not worried by it,' the man explained, 'but the wife says if she catches it she'll leave me, so I thought I'd better come and see you.'

'Well, in the interest of marital harmony, we'd better do something about it,' Nick said. 'Strip down to your underpants so I can see how widespread it's become.'

'But it's only on my arms,' the man protested. 'See the white patches. There are none of them on my body.'

As the man took off his shirt Nick pointed to the irregular pinkish-brown marks on his chest.

'See these,' he said, examining where the rash was worst near the armpit area. 'That's the same thing. On skin exposed to the sun the fungus prevents tanning and you get those white patches. On other parts of your body it shows like these areas.'

The man peered at his chest and nodded.

'Blimey!' he said. 'I hadn't taken much notice of the rest of me. No wonder the wife's upset!'

Nick smiled and opened the drug bag he'd brought with him, searching through its still unfamiliar contents.

'We used to use selenium sulphide for it,' he told the man. 'That's actually the active ingredient in Selsun anti-dandruff shampoo, and many people knew you could rub Selsun onto the white patches and they would go away but they didn't know why.'

'So, do I need anti-dandruff treatment now?' the man joked.

'Not now,' Nick told him, finding what he wanted and straightening up. 'Now we use an anti-fungal tablet, Nizarol. You take one a day with food. Are you on any other medication? Do you take antacids?'

After receiving a negative reply to both questions, Nick wrote the prescribed treatment onto the patient file.

'Only one a day, remember,' he said, handing over the bottle of 200mg tablets. 'Side-effects are rare, but if you experience any nausea or tiredness from them let Belle know and she will contact me.'

Aware that the drug could upset liver function, he made a further note on the file, advising Belle to ask the man about his urine and stool colour if he reported back to her feeling side-effects.

The patient left, and he picked up the next file. As he began reading he realised that here was a case where Jack had made use of the X-ray machine. The man had reported in with severe pains in his shoulder. When an X-ray had ruled out arthritis and other causes of shoulder pain and stiffness, Jack had decided that it must be adhesive capsulitis—the strange phenomenon known to lay people as frozen shoulder.

'Tom Grogan,' the man said, pushing his right hand towards Nick. The limited movement was immediately obvious and, as Nick shook hands then waved him into a chair, he asked the most significant question.

'How's the lack of movement and pain affecting your work?'

Tom shrugged.

'I run the gantry crane and since I've taught myself to use my left hand more work's OK. The pain's been a bit better since Jack started me on anti-inflammatory tablets,' he said, then admitted, 'but I take about four painkillers every day.'

'Not good!' Nick said. He asked Tom to move his arm, and saw him wince when he reached beyond his pain threshold.

'You've been on the Brufen tablets for a month now. Unfortunately the condition usually lasts from six to twelve months regardless of the treatment, then slowly gets better. Jack's note on your file suggests you stick to the tablets for another fortnight. If the pain becomes more severe we'll try a cortisone injection into the shoulder.'

'No miracle cure?' Tom joked, obviously accepting an assessment he'd been given earlier.

'Regretfully, no,' Nick told him. 'But do try to keep up whatever movement you can with it. If you were in the city we'd recommend physio, but out here you're left to your own devices. Could you get hold of a small pulley?'

Tom nodded.

'Then hang it in the doorway of your room, run a length of cord or thin rope through it and use your left hand to help move the right.' He demonstrated what he meant with sling material over the back of a chair.

'Pull down with the left to raise the right, but don't hurt yourself by forcing it too high. Using the pulley, you can get some sideways movement as well. The exercise will help prevent adhesions forming through disuse of the joint.'

'I'll try that,' Tom said. 'Maybe I can cure myself!'

Nick smiled at him, finding that he was impressed by this man and the others who lived in these isolated camps, dragging rare minerals out of the earth. They had a stoicism that reminded him of the early settlers, the men and women for whom the Reverend John Flynn, a minister of religion who had travelled the outback on a camel, had first set up the Flying Doctor Service.

CHAPTER SEVEN

THE third stop-over for the day was in a narrow gorge closer to the coast. The landing was made difficult because of steep ranges rising up on either side of the strip.

'I bet you're glad you've got a fine, clear day for your first flight into Grant's Gully,' Frank remarked as Allysha brought the plane skilfully down into the narrow defile.

'Glad! I'm ecstatic,' she told him, grinning with the sheer delight of a perfect landing. 'I have flown in here twice before, in good weather both times, but I'm pleased to have the practice before the rains set in.'

She eased on the brake and turned around, still smiling, to find Nick watching her. For a moment she thought she saw an answering smile, but when she looked again it had gone and his face was closed and unreadable.

The car waiting for the flight staff bore the logo of the National Parks and Wildlife Service.

'Ben Grant, grandson of the original settlers in the gorge, is now a park ranger,' Jane explained to Nick as they unloaded their gear. She poked her head back into the plane.

'You and Frank come out, Allysha,' she added. 'We have lunch here, and Ben will probably give you a bit of a tour while you're waiting.'

She turned back to Nick.

'Ben shows people around and organises camping

117

trips for the more adventurous tourists who want to
walk up to the head of the gully and explore the cave
system that runs through the mountains,' she told him.

'But I thought it was a mining camp. Surely mining
and National Parks don't mix?' Nick said, remembering
Jack's notes about this particular clinic run.

'Here they do,' Jane assured him. 'The mining lease
predated the declaration of the land as a national park,
but the park rangers oversee the disposal of mine waste
and make certain the run-off from the mine site doesn't
contaminate either the land or the creek that flows
through the gorge.'

Once introductions had been made they set off, Frank
in the front seat to give his sore leg more room and
Allysha wedged between Jane and Nick in the back.

The elation of a successful landing fizzed in her
blood, the excitement rippling through her body.
Squeezed tightly against him, she fancied she felt
Nick's body respond to her reactions. When his thigh
moved slowly and deliberately against hers, a silent
signal of confirmation, her heart went into a frenzy
and she had to concentrate on breathing to prevent the
shallow little gasps of air becoming audible.

Jane's conversation with Ben, calm and prosaic,
seemed to heighten the intensity of her response, turning an ordinary car ride into an interlude of stolen
sensual pleasure.

Then the car stopped and Nick opened the door on
his side.

She turned to look at him, not wanting him to move
without acknowledging that something had happened
between them.

But, 'I'll get the bags,' he said to Jane, then he was
gone, leaving Allysha feeling cold and sickened by an

inescapable sense of shame. What was it about Nick that made her lose all sense of propriety? Of decency? That made her willing to. . . Prostitute herself?

Nick strode away from the car—from Allysha—his body aching with a frustration which might have become obvious if he'd waited one second longer. How could he still want her like this? All right, she might have proved she'd become more responsible. Jack's statement that, after Eddie, she was the best pilot at the Base had forced him to accept this simple fact. And it followed that Peter had proved to be the sobering influence in her life. Peter, who had succeeded in taming her wild rebellion when he, Nick, had failed.

The thought made him feel physically sick, but when he considered the silent messages that had passed between their bodies in the car the sickness magnified itself. He'd accused her once or being unfaithful and, white-faced with anger, she'd denied it. He hadn't believed her at the time but seeing her again after the loneliness of the last twelve months—and the ever-present sense of loss and pain—he'd have been willing to believe anything to get her back.

Only now she was involved with Peter!

And if she was involved with Peter, wasn't what happened in the car tantamount to being unfaithful? In which case she was—

'Straight ahead through that door, Nick.'

Jane's voice saved him from further worthless specu-lation. Maybe he'd imagined what had happened in the car. For all he knew, Allysha had sat there unmoved by his proximity, thinking of nothing more than lunch and a quick jaunt through the National Park.

He walked through the door and saw a table laden

with food, and behind it a smiling young woman in park ranger's uniform.

'I'm Judy Grant, Ben's wife,' she said, stepping forward to greet him. 'We usually feed you all first, then Ben and I will look after your pilot and any passengers while you and Jane check out the locals.'

'The locals include five Grant kids, so there's always something to keep you busy,' Jane explained, but Nick barely heard her. Allysha had walked into the room. The flashing, joyous smile which had set his pulses racing on the plane was gone, and her face was pale and tensely set.

She's not worth worrying about, he told himself, but the thought couldn't banish his concern. When Judy waved him towards the table he picked up a plate and spooned a small helping of every dish onto it. Then he collected cutlery and a napkin, and carried it across to where Allysha had sunk tiredly into a chair.

'Here,' he said, more brusquely than he'd intended. 'Everyone knows this is a tough run for pilots, and you've done magnificently.'

'Have I?' she asked, and looked up into his face for a moment, then looked away. Shock slammed through him. The first thing that had attracted him to Allysha had been her eyes—brown and beautiful, and brimming with a life of their own. They sparkled with mischief, danced with delight, flared with anger, or softened into a mysterious glow when they made love. But today. . .

He reached down and touched her shoulder, stupidly expecting to find it as cold and lifeless as the eyes he'd just glimpsed. Her muscles stiffened beneath his fingers and she seemed to shrink into herself, trying to avoid physical contact without making a scene in front of the others.

His hand dropped away and he walked back to the table to get his own lunch.

'Is Allysha OK? It's a rough trip for all the pilots, this run, and Eddie himself hates the gorge landing,' Jane whispered to him as he haphazardly selected enough food to get his body through the afternoon.

'She'll be OK,' he said, although he didn't believe his own assurance. 'There must be a let-down after you bring off a tricky landing so well.'

Jane nodded and moved away to talk to Judy. Frank and Ben were sitting together, discussing some aspect of mining, and only Allysha sat alone.

I'll have to sit beside her or it will look as if we're ignoring her, he decided, but found himself reluctant to cross the room again. She solved the problem by getting up from her chair and carrying her plate back to the table. She'd eaten some of the food he'd selected, he noticed, but not enough to sustain her.

As she walked out of the room he saw Jane's head signalling him to go after her, but by the time he reached the door she had vanished.

He ate his lunch then worked through the afternoon clinic fighting against the distraction of not knowing where she was, but, after inspecting a variety of infected cuts and grazes, confirming that a swollen ankle was sprained not broken, and prescribing antibiotics for a miner with a throat infection, he would have liked a few more patients.

Instinct told him that he was not ready to face whatever it was that still existed between them, and his heart told him that he couldn't keep punishing her for his own weakness—hurting her because his body craved the relief that only she could offer it.

'I dropped Allysha back at the plane earlier,' Ben

explained when he collected his passengers. 'She wanted to get a weather report and check on fuel or oil or something.'

Nick, knowing that he should have felt relieved to have been spared a repeat of the journey from the plane, was contrarily disappointed. Back on board, he waited until everyone was settled in their seats and then pulled up the door. He was fiddling with the locking device when she came through from the cockpit to check it, and as her arm brushed against his he felt the desire she'd triggered earlier flare back to pulsing life—as real and potent as an electric current.

Allysha concentrated on the take-off. A long walk up the fern-lined gully after lunch had brought little solace, but had calmed her enough to realise that she must forget the nagging attraction she felt for Nick. It had also planted the seed of a new idea.

A determination to prove that she wasn't the useless social butterfly he'd thought her had saved her sanity once before, and now she had decided to tackle a new challenge. She was going to prove that she was the best pilot at the Base. Not second to Eddie, although his hours of experience would always give him an advantage, but the best—the one who would be called out to tricky evac jobs, the one the others were measured against.

Fired by the thought, she accelerated along the tarmac. Every take-off had to be the best! She felt the stomach-shifting lift and watched the ground slide from view.

The banking turn was smoothly executed and she smiled to herself, allowing a little pride to lessen the misery which had enshrouded her.

'You'd beat our mining company pilots hands down,'

Frank said when they were safely on the tarmac at Wyrangi.

'Good flying weather,' she told him, fending off the compliment.

'Rubbish!' he argued. 'They can throw you about in your seat when they land in the most perfect conditions. With you, I could have held a hot cup of tea in my hand all the way and not spilled a drop.'

Allysha felt heat spread colour in her cheeks.

'Well, thanks for the vote of confidence,' she said, wishing she had learned to accept compliments more gracefully. As a child she'd watched people trying to impress her grandmother and their sycophantic remarks and actions had sickened her, although she neither knew the word nor understood her reaction to their behaviour.

'I'll see you at the hospital tomorrow,' Jane said to Nick and then added, as Allysha came down the stairs, 'Enjoy your stay in Wyrangi. I'll see you Friday.'

She turned away from them to hurry into the waiting arms of a burly-looking man. Frank had also been met—thanks to the marvels of the mobile phone network.

'Come up to the hospital on Friday,' Nick called after him. 'I want to show the sister what needs to be done with the dressings.'

As Frank waved his acknowledgement, Allysha closed the plane. The local mechanic was subcontracted to the Service. He would refuel it for her, then take it across to a parking bay, see to the air inlet plugs and chain it down in case a storm blew up.

'Now I've lost my chief guide in Jane, perhaps you could tell me what happens next.'

Nick slung his overnight bag over his shoulder, then

bent to lift the two equipment bags before turning towards her.

'We walk over there,' she said, nodding towards the little shed that served as both passenger and freight terminal. 'There'll be a hospital car waiting for us. Someone drives it out and leaves it here, which saves them waiting around if we're delayed and our waiting around if we're early.'

He was looking at her with a strange intentness, but she remembered her latest resolution and drew strength from it.

'The car's put at your disposal for the two days. The hospital is three kilometres from the hotel, so it's handy if it's too hot or too wet for a walk.'

Nick looked up at the golden orb of the sun, still radiating heat although it was dipping towards the horizon. 'I guess its always one or the other,' he suggested.

'Nearly always,' she agreed.

There should have been other words, he thought. Words that would ease them into a normal conversation, but he couldn't think of any. He turned awkwardly away and continued walking towards the small building.

'We have to go to the hospital first and lock the drugs away,' Allysha reminded him as she collected the car key from the man in charge of the terminal.

He nodded, and let her lead the way towards a small white coupé.

'I'll drive,' he suggested. 'You've done enough for one day.'

She glanced at him, as if surprised he could show compassion. Maybe she had reason to think that, he decided, yet he had congratulated her on her flying and served her lunch.

Allysha unlocked the car, waited while he loaded the two bags and then handed him the keys. As their fingers met she felt the force that had sparked between them earlier, and she realised that this time the challenge would be magnified. Throwing herself into work to forget Nick had been possible when he was thousands of miles away, but when he was working with her? Within touching distance?

She climbed into the car and began to talk—pointing out the road to take, indicating the huge piles of minerals awaiting shipment overseas, the cranes, conveyor belts, and chutes, the other harbour facilities and, finally, the hospital.

'It's a very festive-looking town,' Nick remarked as they drew up outside the hospital.

Allysha absorbed the words and looked around, surprised to notice bright bunting flapping from the hospital guttering.

'It's not usually like this,' she said. 'Were there more coloured flags in town?'

'Everywhere!' Nick confirmed. 'One house even had plastic daffodils stuck into the ground where a garden would normally be. Not quite spring in England, but definitely colourful.'

'Must be something on,' Allysha declared, knowing it was a feeble remark but trying to maintain a pretence at normal conversation.

Nick collected the equipment bags. 'I won't be long,' he said, and walked away.

Looking down towards the town, she saw flags flying over many of the houses and could see the bunting and streamers she'd missed as they drove past.

'It's a prawn festival,' Nick told her when he returned. He started the engine and headed back towards town. 'Evidently it happens every year and, according to Joan—who's the sister-in-charge—all the boats in the gulf fleet try to be here for it. She said it also attracts a number of tourists,' he added dubiously, 'although why anyone would come all this way for a feed of prawns is beyond me.'

'Maybe it's more of an excuse for the locals to get together, like the picnic races further south. Many of the families live on their boats all year round. It would make a change to spend some time in town and catch up with friends from other boats.'

She felt, rather than saw, the look he gave her, and knew immediately what he was thinking. The Allysha he had known would not have thought that through. She would have seen the festival as an excuse to have some fun, without considering the reasons why it had begun or the lives of the people for whom it was intended.

'I had very little chance to learn to think about others,' she said, challenging him before he could voice any surprise. 'I was brought up to think that the world, and everything in it, belonged to me. When you've been given whatever you asked for all your life, you rarely question anything.'

'Poor little rich girl,' Nick murmured, stopping the car in the street outside the hotel.

She spun towards him.

'So it's trite,' she said, eyes snapping out her anger, 'but it also happens to be true. Maybe if I'd gone to school earlier, had the company of other kids, a lot of the behaviour you hated so much would have been knocked out of me there, but I didn't and nothing can change that. My upbringing is part of the person I am.'

She pushed open the car door, reached over into the back seat and grabbed her overnight bag, then marched into the hotel. A volley of whistles and catcalls almost made her turn back and wait for Nick, but she was too upset. Tilting her head defiantly, she walked past the open door of the public bar to the bottom of the stairs and pressed an ancient-looking bell.

'I thought this was a new town built by the mining company,' Nick said, dropping his overnight bag beside hers on the floor and frowning in the direction of the noisy rabble in the bar.

'There's always been a small port here,' she told him, trying to pretend that she was as calm as he was. 'Left over from gold-mining times in the eighteen-hundreds.' She pressed the bell again. 'That's probably when they built the hotel.'

A large, flustered woman arrived and looked at them blankly.

'I'm the new Flying Doctor. I've taken over Jack's clinic run,' Nick said, and the woman's harried expression changed to one of relief.

'I'm Nelly Gervase,' she said. 'For a moment there I thought you were more tourists, and I haven't a bed to spare. In fact, I've already told about seven people they can bunk down on the verandas. If this festival thing keeps growing someone's going to have to build a motel.'

She glanced at Allysha, frowned again and asked, 'Is your friend staying as well? And where's Michael?'

'I'm one of the other pilots,' Allysha explained. 'I've stayed here before with Jack, remember. I'm taking Michael's flights for a few months while he switches to other runs.'

'Of course! I remember you. Pretty name—like Alice,' said Nelly.

'Allysha,' Nick said, but Nelly Gervase was still frowning as she looked from one to the other.

'Yes. . .well. . .' She shifted uncomfortably. 'It's like this, you see. What with the festival and all,' she continued, 'I'd put Jack and Michael into the same room. It's only for these two nights, of course. I was sure they wouldn't mind.'

No! Allysha's mind cried the denial so loudly she was surprised the others hadn't heard it.

'Well, I suppose we can manage to share a room for two nights, Mrs Gervase.'

She heard Nick's voice but couldn't believe what he was saying. She opened her mouth to speak—to say she'd bunk down on the veranda, anywhere—but her throat was dry and her tongue refused to move.

Nelly greeted this decision with a warm smile.

'Oh, you are good! Come on, I'll show you the room. I've put you right at the end, but you might still need earplugs. They're a noisy lot, these fishermen.'

I couldn't control what I feel for him when we were sitting in a car full of people. How am I going to manage sharing a room? The thought held her motionless until Nick took her arm and propelled her up the stairs, following Nelly's retreating form.

'I won't share a room with you,' she snarled at him.

'No?' he muttered coldly. 'I've certainly no intention of ravishing you, so why not?'

Why not, indeed? She searched frantically through her mind for an excuse that wouldn't make her sound like a mid-Victorian virgin—which he knew she wasn't!

'Peter wouldn't like it,' she announced, so pleased

to have found an excuse that her voice sounded triumphant.

'I'm sure Peter would like it even less if I left you unprotected in a town full of men intent on having a ''good time''.'

He said it as if such pleasure was anathema to him, and she remembered how he'd hated the group of wealthy young 'players' of which she'd been a part. Socially irresponsible, he'd called them, and had labelled her—correctly at the time—in the same way.

'Here you are!' Nelly flung open a door at the end of a long corridor. 'Bathroom's four doors back towards the stairs, on the right.' She smiled at Allysha. 'You know there's only one bathroom but it has a good lock on the door, so you use it if you're in there,' she reminded her, before heading back towards the stairs.

'Oh, I didn't tell you. Dinner at seven. Dining-room down the stairs and opposite the bar.'

With a brisk wave of farewell she was gone, and Nick was ushering her into the bedroom.

He threw their two bags on one of the single beds, then turned back to frown at her with total exasperation.

'Jack knew what this town was like. He's surely been here for a festival, so why the hell did he send you?'

'Well, thanks for the vote of confidence,' Allysha snapped, suddenly feeling so tired she could have sat down and cried. And she *never* cried. Then she remembered Nick's kiss and amended the thought to, well, hardly ever.

'I'm having a shower,' she told him, crossing to the bed and unzipping her small bag. The zip stuck, aggravating her more.

'Let me do that,' Nick said, coming to stand beside her and take the bag from her hands.

His closeness escalated her uncertainty, and she held onto the straps. 'I can do it myself,' she argued. 'Contrary to what you persist in believing, I'm not the total incompetent you'd like to think me.'

He tugged the bag from her hands.

'I'm beginning to realise that, Allysha,' he muttered, his voice deep and gruff with a simmering anger. 'Now step aside and let me concentrate on this.'

Her silly heart, immune to all the anger flying around in the atmosphere, skipped a beat. He couldn't concentrate with me so close—surely that must mean something!

Then her head reminded her that she was supposed to be in love with Peter, and she stepped away from the haunting allure of Nick's body. She crossed to the window and looked out at a picture-postcard scene. The fishing boats were drawn up at the old jetty opposite the hotel. As the sun sank beyond the pastel-pink waters of the gulf its last rays touched the paintwork on the sturdy vessels, turning what was probably a grubby grey colour into pristine white.

The same rays caught the nets, slung aloft from spars. They highlighted the deep blue and green colours, making them look like artificial stage dressing. Light glinted off radio masts, flashed off windows and shone on children playing on the jetty, touching the scene with a peculiar vibrancy. Allysha absorbed it all, and felt the beauty soothing her troubled spirit.

Then the sun disappeared and, although the sky retained a reminder of its presence in its fierce orange and magenta splendour, the boats became grey shadows, the nets darkening to black shrouds.

She shivered, and turned away. Nick had fixed the zip but must have had to struggle with it for her clothes were tipped into an untidy pile on the bed, and in his hand he held a nightdress of fine white lawn, lace-trimmed and sewn with pink rosebuds.

It had always been a favourite but, since moving to the humidity of the north, it had become her most worn garment—the slithery silks and satins all discarded in favour of cool cotton. But it was Nick's expression, not her nightdress, that caught her interest. His face was impassive, but she could see the sadness in the tell-tale droop of his lips and in the forward slump of his shoulders.

As she watched he rubbed his thumb across one nubby rosebud and she turned away, feeling that same thumb rub against her tender flesh. She shivered in the hot stillness, then yawned loudly.

'Did you get the zip undone, Nick?' she asked, and turned again to face him, noticing that the nightdress was now neatly folded on the bed.

'Yes! The bag's on the bed,' he said shortly. 'I'm going down for a cool drink; I'll see you at dinner.'

And with that he whisked out the door, moving so quickly that he gave the impression he was running away.

'I've spoken to Joan at the hospital. There's a spare bed in her flat, and she'd be happy for you to stay there.'

Nick greeted her with this news when she walked into the dining-room a little later.

'We'll have dinner, then I'll drive you over.'

Relief and disappointment warred within her, but Allysha managed to smile and say lightly, 'Worried about Peter's reaction if we share a bedroom?'

Nick's face darkened and his lips thinned, but he did not reply, instead waving her towards a table at the back of the big room. As she sat down she noticed the heavy old silver cutlery and snowy white damask napkins, and her eyes gleamed appreciatively. Forgetting she was angry with Nick for organising her life, she turned to him, holding up a shining spoon.

'I'd forgotten about this! Fancy here, of all places, finding beautiful old cutlery and real cloth napkins, not stainless steel and paper. It's like the fishing boats sparkling in the setting sun—something out of another time.'

'It's certainly something out of another time,' he responded wryly, looking around the dark panelled walls of the dining-room. But he, too, slid his fingertips over the cool metal of the cutlery, obviously admiring the economy of design that gave it a functional beauty.

He smiled at her and she relaxed slightly, wondering if a kind of friendship might eventually be possible between them.

'Tell me about your year in America,' she suggested.

He looked at her, startled by the request, then his smile widened.

'I suppose that's as safe a conversation as we're likely to find,' he said, and began to talk about his work on a medical flight team.

Nelly interrupted at one stage to offer them a choice of fresh prawn salad or roast beef.

'I suppose the sensible thing is to have the prawns,' Nick said. 'I presume they are straight off the boats.'

'Caught this morning,' Nelly assured him. 'And the way those blokes are celebrating in there—' she nodded her head towards the bar '—they're the last prawns we'll have for a week or two.'

Allysha agreed that prawns would suit her, and as Nelly departed she looked back at Nick, anxious to hear more of his stories. He turned at the same time and their glances collided, eyes meeting and holding while unspoken thoughts flashed across the air between them.

'Most of the cases we carried were from a primary care unit—like our smaller country hospitals—to a specialist facility, whether paediatric, coronary, neurological, or whatever.'

The words were matter-of-fact medical, so why did she hear music accompanying them? Or was the music in her veins, weaving its way through her blood because at least they were sitting together with a semblance of ease between them—and she could pretend. . .?

The salads arrived—token amounts of wilted lettuce and tired tomato, dominated by a huge pile of prawns.

'Hard to keep salad things up here but I've fresh bread, baked this morning, and that'll go a treat with the prawns.'

'You're not wrong!' Nick agreed. 'It's food for the gods, fresh bread and prawns. We'll do very nicely with that, Mrs Gervase.'

She bustled away and Allysha, embarrassed by the trend of her thoughts, bent her head over her plate and began eating.

The noise in the bar grew louder as their meal progressed.

'If you're finished I'll take you up to get your things, then drive you over to the hospital,' Nick said as she arranged and rearranged the remaining four prawns on her plate. Delicious though they were, she couldn't eat them. She'd had enough—the fact that she was noticing the noise was proof of that.

'Now?'

'Yes, now,' he said tightly, pushing back his chair and standing up.

A series of loud bumps and crashes suggested that furniture was being overturned, and Nick's face grew anxious.

'Come on, Lys,' he urged her, grasping her arm and hurrying her towards the door.

There were yells from across the passageway, and cheers, then a scream that made her blood run cold. Nick stopped and turned, dragging her behind him.

'You wait in the kitchen,' he said. 'I'll get your bag.'

Before she could object she was thrust unceremoniously through the swing door.

'There's trouble in the bar,' he explained to the startled woman.

'There's always trouble in the bar,' she said in a resigned voice. 'Just more during festival time because the more the boys drink the more old arguments they dredge up. If they don't fight amongst themselves they fight the miners on leave here—or unwary tourists who get trapped in the crossfire. Why do you think we hold the festival on the days when your lot are standing by at the hospital?'

Allysha smiled, but she could feel Nick's outrage and knew that it was on her behalf. Half of her was pleased at this cavalier attitude, although she knew she should object and point out that she was well able to take care of herself.

'I'll be back in a few minutes,' he said, and slipped away.

She perched on a stool in the hot kitchen, watching Nelly bustle between the stove and the huge table that dominated the room. The other woman was kneading bread for the next day, and the yeasty smell permeated the air with its strange sensory reminders of home and hearth and family.

Allysha remembered the smell of baking day in the kitchens at home. She had found her way to its source one morning, and had only just begun to absorb the special magic of the yeastiness when her nanny, or her governess—depending on how old she'd been—had come and dragged her away from the 'servants' quarters'.

Nick could mock about her being a 'poor little rich girl' but she wondered if a homely cook might have been a better mother-substitute than the English carers, imported at great expense by her unloving and righteous grandmother.

Lost in her thoughts, she was unaware that more than ten minutes had passed and it was only when Nelly wondered aloud where Nick was that she realised he should have returned by then.

The noise from the bar reached a crescendo of shouts and abuse, making her reluctant to stray from the kitchen, but when Nelly wiped the flour from her hands and muttered, 'Guess I'd better check on the carnage,' she followed her from the kitchen, through the dining-room and across the hall.

The bar resembled a battleground. Chairs and tables were strewn across the floor while half a dozen men staggered about, clutching at the wounded parts of their anatomies.

It was a battle scene, but a quiet one. Then cries from beyond the old swing doors drew their attention. The war had shifted outside.

CHAPTER EIGHT

IT WAS an hour before peace was restored, and then only through the intervention of a car-load of sober young tourists. Arriving at the hotel with the intention of joining the festivities, they were soon drafted into a makeshift posse by the local policeman. Once the most militant of the warriors had been forcibly restrained, the heat of the encounter diminished.

Nelly and Allysha were kept busy staunching blood that seemed to flow as freely as the alcohol had a little earlier. When the fight was finally stopped, three of the young men helped the policeman load the worst of the conscious aggressors into his sturdy covered truck and agreed to accompany him to the station.

'There are only two beds in the lock-up so they can continue their fight over who sleeps where. With any luck, they might all end up unconscious and the rest of us will get some rest,' the policeman said bitterly to Nick. 'Ring me at the station if you've any problem with your patients.'

He glanced around at the bruised and battered men and women, sitting or lying on the ground.

'You won't have room to keep many of them at the hospital. Let's hope the pain is sobering them up fast, and those who have homes will be able to find them. Can you manage, or will I drop this lot off and come back?'

'I think I can,' Nick told him and Allysha, hearing his voice, looked up from where she knelt beside a woman, who was bleeding profusely from a scalp wound.

The neat and tidy doctor had disappeared, she noticed. He looked as dirty and fight-roughened as all the others who'd been caught in the fray, whether fighting or trying to stop it. Yet she sensed a satisfaction in him, and thought she caught a gleam of excitement in his dark eyes.

'I'll load as many as possible into the hotel Range Rover, and the two lads who've been helping can take a few more in their car. I saw Mrs Gervase here some-where—she'll know who's staying at the hotel and can help them up to bed if they don't need stitching or plastering. Mrs Gervase!' he repeated and then, as Allysha watched, his body stiffened and he turned to look around more intently. His gaze swept across her the first time, but then he searched again and she fancied she saw his shoulders slump a little with relief.

Some fancy! A moment later he was striding towards her like an avenging god of retribution.

'I thought I told you to stay inside!' he fumed, glaring down at her.

She lifted one hand, an automatic gesture to ward off his anger, and he paled and dropped down to kneel beside her, muttering swear words she couldn't believe he knew.

'Show me your hand,' he ordered and, confused by the anger that seemed to radiate from his body, she lifted her hand to him.

'The other hand!' he snapped, and she moved it from the pad that was pressed against the dazed woman's head. Nick opened her fingers, his own hand trembling. Allysha saw the blood on her palm and understood his reaction.

'It's not my blood, Nick,' she said softly, and he turned and looked into her eyes. She read his relief, and something else that made her heartbeats flutter erratically.

For a moment the world slipped out of focus, then someone called for the doctor and he squeezed the hand he still held before standing up and waving an acknowledgement.

'I'll be with you in a moment!' he called, then turned back to her to ask, 'Are you OK to drive?'

He lingered by her side after he'd examined the woman's wound, and she felt that he was reluctant to move. Was his body clamouring with the same excitement hers felt? Or were her palpitations simply a hangover of adrenalin from her involvement in the fight?

'I'm OK,' she quavered, amazed that her voice was working at all.

'If the woman can walk help her to the hospital car,' he said gently. 'I'll get one of my helpers to take another mobile patient with you, and he can drive the car back here in case we need more transport.'

He hesitated, as if he wanted to say more, then frowned—but not at her, she thought—and walked over to where a small group was gathering around an injured man.

Allysha helped the woman to her feet.

'Put your arm around my shoulders and lean on me,' she told her. 'The car's at the back of the hotel. I'll drive you up to the hospital. You need a couple of stitches in a cut.'

The young man arrived, accompanied by a teenage lad, white-faced with pain and holding gingerly to his forearm.

'Drive nice and steady, Miss,' the young man said. 'Doc says his arm's broken. It must be hurting like hell!'

She 'drove steady', and was glad when they reached the hospital. It was a low-set building with a wide covered veranda along the front. Joan came running out to greet them.

'Nelly phoned to tell me to make up all the beds,' she said, helping the woman out of the car. 'Was it that bad?'

'It wasn't good,' Allysha told her. 'Do you have Jane's number? I think you and Nick will need all the help you can get.'

She handed the car keys to the young man, then followed Joan and the patients into what was normally a waiting-room at the small hospital.

'There's an office of sorts through there,' Joan said, indicating a door on the left of the short corridor. 'Jane's number is written on a card above the calendar. Would you mind ringing her while I X-ray this arm? When you've finished my flat is out the back if you want to go on out there and get some rest.'

'Rest?' Allysha said, smiling at the other woman. 'These are only two of the walking wounded; there must be another ten of them, and at least four knocked out completely. I'll phone Jane, then come and help. You can think of something useful for me to do while you're taking your pictures.'

She walked through to the office, noticing a four-bed ward off to the right, and a room that was obviously the X-ray room and theatre beyond the office on the left. She made her phone call, apologising to Jane and explaining what had happened.

'There are three other numbers under Jane's,' Joan

called from the corridor before she had time to leave
the desk. 'One retired nurse, who acts as my relief when
we're busy, and two aides. I suppose we'd better get
them all up here.'

Allysha nodded and picked up the phone again.

'I've got onto one aide, and the nurse will be back
tomorrow,' she explained when her phone calls were
completed. 'According to her son, she and her husband
have been out on their boat for a few days but I've left
a message for her to contact you,' she reported.

Joan was stitching the woman's wound and the teenager was sitting back in a chair, still holding his arm.
She sighed philosophically.

'Well, if you're going to work in my hospital you'd
better have a wash,' she suggested. 'You look as if
you've been in the thick of things. Bathroom's opposite
the office. You'll find paper towels in the cabinet above
the sink.'

The mirror confirmed Joan's observation, and
Allysha scrubbed the dirt from her face, hands and arms,
smoothed her ruffled hair and went back out. By the
time she emerged another car-load of patients had
arrived, and a short, dark woman was bustling around.

'I'm Mary, the aide you spoke to on the phone. Only
live over the road,' she explained. 'Now, you stick with
me.' She handed Allysha a stack of four stainless-steel
bowls and a kidney dish. 'I'm going to clean people
up a bit, dress any wounds that don't need stitching
and see if I can get rid of the malingerers who've come
looking for a comfortable bed.'

She pushed a small trolley in front of her to the
veranda where an assortment of men and women were
slumped on the floor or propped against the wall, hold-

ing various parts of their bodies and groaning almost in unison.

Mary moved along the row, cleaning and dressing wounds and ignoring the yelps of protest as antiseptic bit into damaged tissues. Allysha caught the discarded swabs in her kidney dish, and passed whatever Mary wanted from the trolley.

'Basin,' Mary yelled, and she retrieved one of the basins she'd put on the bottom shelf and thrust it forward as a man gulped, then rid himself of his last few drinks.

Allysha's stomach churned rebelliously, but she fought her nausea and held the dish steady while he retched and coughed.

'Get rid of it and come straight back,' Mary told her. 'There's more than one must be feeling squeamish by now.'

She hurried towards the bathroom, just as Nick and another of the tourists were carrying an unconscious man onto the veranda. His eyes asked a question, and she smiled.

'I'm only doing maid's duties,' she assured him, flourishing the odorous basin. 'I won't start on surgery until tomorrow.'

He hesitated for a moment, then smiled back at her and she felt an easing of her spirit.

The mayhem continued until late into the night.

'OK,' Mary finally announced when the veranda was clear of bodies. 'Let's see how things are going inside this place. We'll start by making coffee and sandwiches for the workers. Can't have the doctor keeling over with exhaustion, now can we?'

Allysha followed obediently. The waiting-room had been turned into another ward, the chairs removed and mattresses placed on the floor. The teenager, his arm now encased in plaster, was asleep in one and a burly man, his head and arms swathed in bandages, lay motionless in another.

Glancing at the third occupant, Allysha was surprised to see a familiar face. Frank—the miner from Twin Mountain—was moving restlessly, trying to get comfortable with his bad leg propped on a frame at the end of his mattress.

'How did you get involved? You said you were a non-drinker,' Allysha whispered, kneeling to help him replace a cushion that had fallen from the frame.

'Went down to collect my girlfriend when she finished work and found all hell breaking loose. Tried to get her away but some stupid fisherman reckoned he fancied her and I had to knock him out, and now Doc says I've probably busted my knuckles and might have to go back to the Bay with you lot.'

He sounded so disgusted with himself that she chuckled.

'It's a wound of chivalry,' she told him, patting the heavily bandaged hand. 'Gained protecting your girl-friend's honour.'

'A wound of stupidity, more like,' a deep voice said, and she spun around to see Nick looking down at her.

'You should be in bed,' he added, reaching out a hand to help her up. 'It's after midnight and you've had a long day.'

His voice was rough with the fatigue he wouldn't admit to, but there was concern for her in his face and it teased its way into her body and made her feel. . .

She didn't know how she felt! Except that she wanted to stand where she was for ever, close to Nick, one hand warm in his. His fingers moved against her skin,

sending silent messages along her nerves. It's a soothing, caring touch, that's all, her head reminded her, but
the heat building inside her was not the proper response
to reassurance.

'You there, Doc?'

An urgency in the words broke the spell, and Nick
dropped her hand and walked away—out onto the
veranda where the policeman had another patient.

Nick and the policeman carried the man through to
the theatre. Allysha followed, looking for the kitchen
and Mary. Beyond the theatre a covered walkway led
across to Joan's flat and beside it, she discovered, the
hospital kitchen.

'Built it out here to keep the heat and smells away
from the hospital,' Mary explained. They made a plate
of sandwiches, and set pots of tea and coffee on the
table. 'Go and tell them there's food and hot drinks in
here,' Mary said, and Allysha walked back to the ward.

Joan was there, bent over a restless patient. Allysha
passed on her message, then crossed the passage to the
theatre. Through the glass panel in the door she could
see Nick and Jane working on their patient, while the
policeman hovered just inside the room.

She pushed open the door slightly and, as he turned
to see who it was, she whispered, 'Hot drinks and food
in the kitchen when these two finish. Could you let
them know?'

He nodded, but Nick must have heard her voice for
he looked up and she saw his eyes, framed by cap and
mask and dark with something she couldn't understand.

'Find a bed and get some sleep, Allysha,' he said
sharply. 'That's an order. If I have to transfer any of
these patients I don't want a delay because my pilot
isn't fit for work.'

For a microsecond she felt affronted by his tone, then she realised he was calling on her professionalism. She had proved helpful in the crisis, emptying basins and bedpans, but he might need her flying skill in the morning and she had to be ready. She glanced at her watch and nodded.

Nick watched her walk away, and shook his head. For twelve months he'd been reminding himself that she was a spoilt, selfish, self-indulgent socialist. She was funny—yes! Intriguing? Definitely! Seductive? Don't think about it! And fascinating beyond words! But she lacked compassion, he'd reminded himself; had no understanding of other people's lives and problems. And she was without commitment to anything, without ambition or a sense of duty—the things that were so important to him!

'There's a fluttery sound in his chest but no shift in the trachea, and no obvious respiratory distress.'

Jane's observations brought his attention back to the patient.

He held his stethoscope to the injured chest and listened. The man had multiple rib fractures, which had damaged the bony integrity of the chest wall and thrown the pressure gradients within it out of balance.

'You can have a flail chest injury without a leakage of blood or air into the chest cavity from some internal damage,' he muttered, more to himself than to Jane, 'only it's rarely that easy, and instinct tells me not to believe in miracles.'

'But now we've padded out the caved-in portion we've stopped the abnormal movement of that part of the chest. Won't he breathe normally?'

Nick nodded, concerned about possible internal damage and trying to visualise what could be happening in the man's chest. He suspected that the man had been flung against the bar early in the fight. He'd walked away from the fight at that stage, and only sought help at the police station when he'd sobered up enough to feel the agonising pain in his ribs.

The multiple fracture meant that the injured part of the chest moved with each breath, being drawn inward on inspiration and pushed outward on expiration. The pain must have been excruciating!

He was now asleep, thanks to strong pain relief, and his ribs were splinted to hold the padded dressings in place and restore the dynamics of respiration, but had blood vessels been damaged? Was his circulation suffering under increased pressure on the heart and the great vessels beneath the midline of his chest? He checked the pulse oximeter and told himself not to worry, but he couldn't banish an uneasiness that all was not well with his patient.

'There are no beds in the ward, so we'll put up the rails and leave him here,' he said, after a thorough secondary examination had revealed no further cause for his niggling concern. 'Will you watch him while I grab some food and coffee, then I'll come back and sit up with him? If I have to do an emergency chest decompression at least I'll have him on the operating table.'

He walked away, half hoping to find Allysha in the kitchen. But the work ethic he had been so reluctant to acknowledge in her had sent her straight to bed, according to Mary, who blamed him that the 'poor girl' hadn't even had a sandwich.

Trying not to think of the 'poor girl', he ate sandwiches, drank a cup of coffee and then a glass of water, knowing that dehydration would accentuate his

tiredness if he didn't keep enough fluids in his body.
Before relieving Jane he checked on the other new
admissions, assuring himself that they all seemed stable
and that complications during the next few hours were
unlikely.

'There's no sign of respiratory distress but his chest
percussion sounds are dull,' Jane told him. 'It sounds
like fluid accumulating there.'

Haemothorax! he thought.

'It's probably blood from soft tissue damage. I'll
aspirate him,' Nick said, watching the man's chest rise
and fall as he breathed in an oxygen mix through the
mask over his mouth and nose. Jane waited while he
listened to the man's chest, tapping lightly until
he found the dullness she had heard.

'You go and get some food, then find a bed. You'll
have to fly out with this patient—and possibly one of
the men with concussion. This X-ray machine is good
but I'm not certain it would pick up a hairline skull
fracture, so I think I'll send him to town.'

'I'll use Joan's bed,' Jane said. 'That way I'll be
here for the flight. She'll be on duty until her relief
comes in the morning, so she won't need it.'

As she left the room Nick crossed to the equipment
cupboard. He sorted through the needles, seeking one
with a large bore, 14 or 16 gauge, through which he
could withdraw any accumulated blood. Back with his
patient, he counted down the ribs and chose the eighth
interspace, cleaned the area carefully and anaesthetised
it before inserting the needle. Using a large syringe, he
aspirated the accumulated blood, measuring it and
noting the 400ml on the man's chart. More than
1500ml was considered massive haemorrhage—so the
relatively small amount was reassuring.

The chest percussion sounded better, but the nagging uncertainty remained. Once again he considered his patient, working visually at first from head to toes, then touching him, palpating, hoping that his fingers might tell him what he was missing. And finally he looked at the machines. The patient's heart showed strong regular rhythm, blood pressure slightly elevated but not exceptional, pulse steady, respiration even.

'There's nothing else,' he assured himself and he left his patient and walked through the hospital again, checking on the others.

'I've got onto the harbour master,' Joan told him as he passed the office. 'They keep the State Emergency Service vehicle down at their facility. It's fitted out to take stretchers, and we use it when we need an ambulance.'

'Can he have it here at first light?' Nick asked, and Joan nodded.

'Sunrise is about five-thirty he tells me. He'll make sure it's here by then.'

'By which time our nurse and pilot will have had at least four hours' sleep,' Nick remarked.

'More than you and I will have had,' Joan reminded him, then hurried away as someone called to her from the ward.

Nick found one of the chairs from the waiting-room out on the veranda and carried it through to the theatre. He checked his patient again and then sat down, telling himself he could afford to sleep for fifteen minutes.

Cat-napping through the night had left him feeling decidedly worse than having had no sleep at all, he decided as dawn lightened the sky outside the window. He checked his patient yet again before crossing to the bathroom, where he splashed cold water over his face, rinsed out his mouth, then swore as the paper towel caught on his beard stubble, leaving damp white shreds all over his chin.

'You look dreadful,' Joan told him when he walked into the office to phone Jack.

'I feel worse,' he told her, dialling the now-familiar number.

Jack assimilated the information surprisingly quickly for someone woken before daybreak.

'I'd send the chap with the injured hand to town, as well as the other two,' he said. 'Allysha will let the Base know her ETA and we'll have an ambulance there to meet her. Now, how many others will you have to keep in hospital over there?'

Nick ignored the strange twinge that hearing Allysha's name caused, and did a quick mental count.

'We've two we should be able to discharge this morning, which will leave three.'

'And how many did Joan have on the surgery list for you? How many of them would you expect to have to keep overnight?'

Nick pulled forward the list that Joan had left on her desk.

'One tonsillectomy—he's a young adult and could be prone to bleeding so I'd like to keep an eye on him. One baby with an umbilical hernia—should be no problem there. Carpal tunnel, ditto, a few BCCs and a wart removal. We'll have a bed for the tonsillectomy, and he should be the only overnighter.'

'I'm on call so I could come out and bring a nurse with me,' Jack suggested. 'That way you could get some sleep while I do the surgery.'

'I think that's the most sensible idea,' Nick agreed.

'Will you stay over and take me back after tomorrow's clinic?'

There was a moment's silence, then Jack replied, 'No, I'll fly back to town this afternoon—if there's not another emergency call to pull me out earlier. Allysha can unload her passengers, collect another nurse and go back to Wyrangi this afternoon. That way you'll have a plane on the ground in case there's another riot.'

'Don't even think about it!' Nick groaned, and heard Jack chuckle before the line was disconnected.

'Trouble?'

He was replacing the receiver as she spoke, and his head jerked up at the sound of Allysha's voice.

'No more than we can handle,' he assured her, then smiled and shook his head as her weird attire registered. 'New uniform for pilots, is it?'

Allysha looked down at the bright floral shift she'd borrowed from Joan to replace her soiled uniform. Belted around her waist to reduce its size, it fell in gaudy, voluminous folds around her slight frame.

'You never did get my overnight bag from the hotel room,' she reminded him. 'I've had to make do.'

'You'd look good to me in a wheat sack,' he said, and the tired resignation in his voice cut into her heart. She stepped forward and reached out across the desk to touch him, but he sat back in his chair and rubbed his hand across unshaven chin. 'Sorry! Unwelcome personal remark! Put it down to lack of sleep.'

Allysha felt a wall come up between them and let her hand drop.

'If I drive out to the airport in the hospital car is there some conveyance to get your patients out there? If I leave now I can do the pre-flight checks and be ready to take off when they arrive.'

He looked up at her and she saw shadows chase across his eyes before he nodded.

'Take the car; Joan has organised a vehicle for the patients. If you leave the car at the airport Jack can use it to drive to the hospital when he arrives.'

It was an abrupt dismissal but she welcomed it, feeling silly tears she didn't want him to see gathering in her eyes.

It's tiredness, she told herself as she moved away from him, hating to admit to a weakness she despised.

'Did I judge you too harshly?' he muttered as she turned to leave the room.

She spun around, unable to believe what he was asking. What could she say after all this time? She suppressed the anger that was her immediate reaction; the anger that rose from the knowledge that it was too late.

'Not really,' she answered quietly. 'My decision to go to that ball was everything you said it was—the wilful, childish gesture of a spoilt brat who hadn't got what she wanted. As to the rest—' she shrugged '—I think a little trust on both our parts might have helped.'

Now's not the time for this conversation, her aching heart told her. He's tired and disorientated—likely to say things he doesn't mean. And I'm likely to read more into them than I should!

'I've got to go,' she whispered, and he didn't try to stop her when she turned and walked away.

Out at the airport she unchained the plane, leaving the chocks in place while she removed the plugs from the air-vents, the cover from the pilot tube and did her visual pre-flight check. A large SES vehicle drew up as she opened the door and, while she put on the brake and removed the chocks, Jane supervised the loading of their patients.

Once again she felt a split within herself. On one level she was working professionally, using all the skill and competence she had acquired over the years. But on another level an argument raged, and she wondered if professionalism was enough to keep the re-ignited flames of her passion for Nick in check.

Or would she need to? her heart whispered. Didn't his question mean that she still meant something to him? Had he lied when he said she'd killed his love?

Or did his question stem from left-over lust? A physical thing that flickered between them like the dying flutter of a fire, clouding the issues and confusing both mind and body?

The plane lifted with effortless ease, and she looked down at the blue-grey water of the gulf. The fishing fleet was pastel-coloured in the early morning light, without the flagrant beauty stolen from the sun's setting rays.

Was our love like that sunset? she wondered. Too rich and hot and vibrant—too wildly coloured to be real or sustainable?

She put aside her unproductive thoughts and brought her patients safely home.

Eddie was at the airport.

'Nice dress!' he said, grinning at her strange garb. 'Leave the plane for Jeff and come into the hangar for a chat.'

A chat with Eddie usually meant something had been left undone. Surely she'd filed all her flight reports?

'Did the fight out at Wyrangi worry you? Were you frightened you could have been hurt?'

Allysha smiled and shook her head.

'They were far too busy fighting each other to worry about me, and I had Nelly Gervase by my side all the time,' she assured him. 'Why?'

It was Eddie's turn to smile.

'Jack's never been happy about a woman pilot on that run, and I've argued that I won't discriminate on the matter of sex. That's got to cut both ways, Allysha. I hire pilots on ability, and hired you because you were the best young pilot I'd seen in a long time. But, having done that, I can't mollycoddle you.'

She sighed and shook her head.

'I've already had this conversation with Jack,' she said. 'I'd be the first to complain if I thought you were giving work that should be mine to one of the men because he is a man. I kept right out of the way while the fight was raging, and only appeared for the mopping-up operations. I'd be disappointed if you bowed to some silly whim of Jack's and took me off the route.'

Which sealed her fate as Nick's pilot until the next re-shuffle!

'I think it was a bit of extra pressure from Nick on the phone this morning that started Jack worrying again.'

The information hit her like a physical force, but it strengthened her determination. She would stay on that run whether Nick liked it or not—and she would prove her professionalism by learning to ignore his presence altogether.

As she drove home later she knew she could achieve the first resolve, but admitted to herself that the second was probably impossible. Already her body was missing the sweet agony of having him nearby, and her mind kept returning to Wyrangi as she tried to visualise what he would be doing.

CHAPTER NINE

THE resolve that had awakened in Grant's Gully, and been strengthened by Eddie's conversation, carried Allysha through not only her return to Wyrangi but the succeeding weeks. She was kept busy with a spate of evacuation and emergency flights. With the Wet Season closing in, flights became more difficult, challenging her determination to be 'the best'.

The survivors of the battle of the prawn festival had all returned home, even Rod Weller—the man who had been brought in late in the night with the chest injury.

'Nick worried about him all night, certain there was something else wrong,' Jane had told her. 'So much so that he put a huge question mark on the file that accompanied the patient to hospital.'

'Wouldn't a simple note saying, "I'm worried about this man," have had the same effect?' she'd asked, and Jane had laughed.

'Nick felt they could miss a little note in A and E, but defacing the precious file would certainly gain attention.'

Allysha had chuckled.

'And did they find anything else?'

'Myocardial contusion. When he was thrown against the bar the heart was compressed between the sternum and the backbone. Fortunately it was only a small lesion and the bleeding didn't lead to blood accumulating in the pericardial sac, which would have caused a major panic. But Nick's question mark meant the doctor at

the hospital ordered X-rays, scans and ultrasound—the
works—and put the chap on a heart monitor from
the start.'

Allysha had felt a stupid, contrary burst of pride in
Nick's percipience—then tried to pretend that she'd
have felt the same if it had been Peter or Jack!

As they flew back to Wyrangi six weeks after Nick's
first trip to the mining camps he came up to the cockpit
and dropped into the seat beside her.

'You're looking tired,' he said. 'Have you been playing up while Jane and I've been working?'

He spoke in a light, joking manner but she knew that
he was puzzled about what she did during the two days
in the small town. Since that first visit they had avoided
any opportunity for intimacy, sitting together as colleagues in the dining-room of the hotel if they happened
to be eating at the same time, but nothing more.

'I'm fine,' she told him, although the sniffle that had
started a few days ago had turned into a cold, and even
in the pressurised King Air her ears were aching.

'Well, you don't look fine!' he said argumentatively.
'You've been flying far too many emergency flights,
on top of the strain of the mining clinics. I'm going to
speak to Eddie about it.'

She refused to turn and look at him, although she
was surprised by the vehemence in his voice. Looking
at Nick started all the old tremors, and she was putting
that behind her.

'I had my regular physical a fortnight ago,' she told
him, staring out at the dirty grey clouds through which
they were flying. 'There's nothing wrong with me!'

'I don't believe you, Lys,' he stated, and the old
nickname stabbed through her skin, sharp as any knife.

'You're pale, and the circles under your eyes are nearly black.'

Because I haven't slept properly for over six weeks, she wanted to yell, but she bit back the reaction and muttered about having a bit of a cold.

'Well, I'm glad it's not because you're two-timing Peter with some bloke in Wyrangi,' he growled, and this time fury made her turn and glare at him.

'My relationship with Peter is none of your business,' she snapped, 'and, contrary to what you want to believe, I never "two-timed" you, Nick Furlong. You leapt to that conclusion because it suited you. I might have been outrageous and silly, and all the other things you called me, but what worried you wasn't my behaviour but that the wonderful, dedicated, sensible Flying Doctor you thought yourself could be attracted to such a total washout!'

She hesitated a moment, expecting him to refute her accusation, but then the anger that had fired her outburst flamed higher and she couldn't have stopped the words escaping even if she'd tried.

'Do you think I didn't know how much you hated yourself for being drawn to me? Did you think I couldn't feel it when you touched me sometimes, and see it when you looked at me, frowning while you tried to work out where you'd gone wrong—to be saddled with such a frivolous nothing?'

'I loved you, Lys,' he said gravely, but she looked away, not wanting to see his eyes in case they repeated the message in the past tense of the verb.

'And hated yourself for it,' she said, her voice tight with the emotion that choked her lungs and filled her throat. 'Hated yourself so much it was easy to jump to conclusions; easy to say all the things you'd been wanting to say, and walk away from me for ever!'

She could feel his anger stirring now, but she checked her instruments and pretended that her attention was focused on the plane.

'And what conclusion would you have reached if our roles had been reversed?' he demanded. 'You fly out now to ''hangover'' scenes, to the aftermath of picnic races or those ridiculously named Bachelor and Spinster Balls. I know the wild ones are only a minority, but aren't you sickened by the sight of people suffering from over-indulgence, of bodies strewn carelessly around the place—half-naked after casual sex with strangers?'

'My body wasn't strewn anywhere half-naked,' she argued. 'It was tucked, fully clothed, into a single sleeping bag under a tarpaulin that had been pulled up to keep the dew off.'

'Tucked in beside a man who did not look fully clothed and had one arm slung across you!' Nick rasped out the words as if the contempt he'd felt that morning was still alive and well in his heart.

'There were at least three women and about six other men under that tarpaulin, and I hadn't slept with any of them,' she reiterated stubbornly, 'and, what's more, I think you probably realised that. I was silly, and easily led, and irresponsible,' she added, her voice husky with the memory of the pain of his rejection, 'but you, of all people, should have known I wasn't promiscuous.'

She turned away from her perusal of the instruments and looked into his eyes, then, drawing a deep breath, she added, 'I think you used that night as an excuse to escape from something you'd decided you couldn't handle; to escape from an engagement you'd had doubts about all along.'

It was his turn to look away, but Allysha thought she'd read the answer in the slump of his shoulders and the tired bowing of his head.

'Couldn't you understand my doubts?' he asked. 'There was I, a kid from the inner suburbs who'd grown up in a housing commission house with working-class parents and five siblings. I'd been blessed with enough brains to get through University as a doctor, and I had the determination to work hard and succeed at my job— but that was all, Lys.

'What was I supposed to offer one of the wealthiest women in the state? Why should she have been attracted to me? Unless I was another whim? A novelty? Another bit of fun?'

He paused, but she couldn't speak.

'Maybe I did seize on the ball as an excuse. Maybe I was so scared you would tire of me and dash off at another tangent that I grabbed at the chance to end it before you could.'

Again his voice stopped, and she heard him dragging air into his lungs.

'Maybe I believed it would hurt less that way,' he rasped, then he stood up and made his way back into the cabin.

Echoes of his words sounded in her ears long after he had gone, melding with the pain and making her feel curiously light-headed. The radio's incessant chatter impinged on her consciousness, and she dragged her attention back to the flight and radioed her ETA. They landed safely and on time, but as she taxied towards the hangar she wondered if her slight cold had turned into something worse or if the hazy feeling was delayed shock from Nick's unexpected attack.

She sat in the cockpit, hearing the noises that told

her Jane and Nick were taking their gear off the plane.

'I'll wait till they're gone,' she whispered to herself, and leant forward, folding her arms across the instrument panel so that she could rest her aching head on something soft.

Jane called goodbye, and she managed an appropriate response. The medical staff usually left before she did after clinic runs, only waiting around for the pilot if it was dark or if they had shared transport to the airport.

'I'll put her away for you!'

Jeff's voice, but still she couldn't lift her head and leave the plane. It was as if all will and energy had drained from her body, leaving her limp and boneless.

'Your "bit of a cold" is obviously the flu. Come on, I'll drive you home.' Nick's voice—and the last person she wanted driving her home!

Move! she ordered her aching body. Cautiously she lifted her head and then, ignoring the thumping protest in her temples, she pushed herself out of her seat.

'I can drive myself,' she mumbled, although she was beginning to wonder if she could get herself successfully out of the plane.

'How long have you been feeling ill?' he asked, and she flinched away from the anger in his voice.

He must have seen the movement for a string of curses followed and, as she closed her eyes and rested her burning forehead on the cool metal of the hatch above the open door, she felt his hands reach out and touch her.

'I can drive myself,' she repeated, pulling away from his touch.

'Stopping to faint every few minutes, I suppose,' he growled, moving so that his arm was around her shoulders. 'Why didn't you tell someone you were feeling ill? Why did you fly when you were as sick as you obviously are? Didn't you realise you were—?'

'Endangering lives?' she interrupted as he steered her towards the parked cars. 'Well, I wasn't and I didn't! I've flown with a worse cold than this, but this time my ears must have been affected by the pressure change. They began to ache as we climbed, but I was fit enough to fly.'

'And if you'd fainted while you were at the controls?'

'We were on autopilot,' she muttered, compelled to argue with him although she was feeling sicker by the minute.

He opened the passenger door on his car, and eased her into the seat. New-car smell assailed her nostrils.

'That would have been a big help when we landed,' he said stiffly, climbing in beside her and starting the engine.

She began to wish that she could faint! How could she tell him that she'd felt all right until he'd brought up the past; until he'd verbally attacked her with what had happened between them, and forced her to defend herself at last? That had been the final straw, she thought fuzzily, no camel's back would have been able to withstand it! Certainly her aching head hadn't been able to cope. She'd held on until she'd got them all safely home, then had let the tide of sickness and despair wash over her.

'Will I take you to Peter's?' Nick asked, and she turned to stare at him, unable to understand the question.

'Why on earth would you take me to Peter's?' she muttered, pressing her fingers against her forehead in an effort to halt the pounding.

'Because you're not capable of looking after yourself

at the moment,' Nick said in the rigid kind of voice he had always used when she'd upset him. 'I would have thought he'd be the obvious person to play doctor, or nurse, or whatever you need.'

'Take me home, Nick,' she whispered, too sick to try to untangle the conversation. 'All I need is an aspirin and a good night's sleep. I'd rather be on my own.'

She closed her eyes, unable to argue any more, and gave in to the gentle motion of the car. As he pulled up outside the door of The Bay Towers she opened her door and got out before he'd turned off the engine. She bent down and leaned in.

'Thanks for the lift. I'll be OK,' she assured him, and hurried towards the foyer of the building.

'Surprise!'

The raucous shout hammered in her head and Allysha wondered who was being surprised, then a crowd of people blocked her path and she lifted her heavy eyelids and tried to focus on the scene. She saw Brent first, then a motley assortment of the group with whom she had once partied.

'You wouldn't come to see us, so we came to see you,' a husky voice said, and she turned to see Abby, so thin that her bones were outlined by her skin. She still wore the most outrageous of the Paris fashions, Allysha registered vaguely.

'That's great,' she said weakly, 'but I'm—'

'Sick is the word, Allysha!'

Nick's voice rattled up her spine.

'So, the worthy doctor reappeared, did he?' Brent's voice this time. 'And the other one was so much handsomer. I could have gone for him myself.'

It was like slime, Allysha thought hazily. And when you got close to it, it covered you as well.

'Are you going up to make your own way up to bed, or shall I carry you?'

The loud demand brought a chorus of noisy derision from her erstwhile 'friends', and Allysha knew that she had to move before the disturbance brought complaints from the man on duty at the desk.

'I'll be all right,' she said to Nick, then she turned towards the others and smiled vaguely.

'It's—ah—nice to see you all,' she said weakly, good manners hiding the truth of her despair at their reappearance. 'But not today. I'm feeling terrible; I'll catch up soon.'

Her hand lifted in a sketchy wave and she headed towards the lifts, pleased to find the doors opening immediately she pressed the button.

She stepped inside, registered her floor and slumped against the wall, eyes closed as she remembered. She had broken with these people and told Abby, the only one who might have qualified as a close friend, why she wanted to get away. But Abby hadn't understood her need to prove herself; her desire to discover if she was capable of doing more than 'having fun'.

'Do they come up often?'

Her eyes flew open and Nick's face, dark with the intensity of his anger, filled her vision.

'What are you doing here?' she whispered as the last drops of energy drained from her body.

'You left your case in the car.'

He lifted his hand, and she saw the case she'd taken to Wyrangi dangling from his fingers. She shook her head, unable to remember carrying it off the plane, but the movement made the aching worse so she closed her eyes again until she felt the lift stop.

'Come on,' he said gruffly, easing his arm around her shoulders again and helping her into the small foyer. 'I'm not leaving until you're tucked safely into bed. Now, where are your keys?'

She reached into her handbag that, thankfully, was slung across her shoulder where it should be, and fumbled for the cool metal of the keys.

'Let me do that,' he said, impatiently pulling her fingers out of the way and lifting the weight of her bag so that he could peer into its depths.

The jangle of keys told her that he'd found them and, as he bent to try each one in the lock, she saw the little strands of dark hair curling against his neck, the way they did when his hair needed cutting.

It was so familiar—so dear—that her fingers moved to touch them, but he straightened up and the moment was lost.

'Come on,' he urged, as if she was a duty he wanted done with as soon as possible. 'You get into bed; I'll fix you some tea and toast. Do you keep aspirins or cold tablets in the house?'

'I'll be all right,' she protested weakly, but the thought of getting into bed was so seductive that she turned towards the bedroom. She stripped off her uniform, pulled on a comfortable old towelling robe and collapsed on the bed, her eyes closing against the throbbing ache in her temples that kept time with the pounding beat of her heart.

She heard Nick muttering about food and tablets, then about pulse and temperature and thought she felt his hands—touching her, lifting her, telling her to do this and do that.

*   *   *

'Feeling better?'

A soft, cool voice, not hot and rasping and angry as Nick's had been!

She eased her sticky eyelids apart and peered towards the direction of the voice.

'Leonie?'

The base manager smiled at her.

'Nick stayed last night,' Leonie explained, 'then was called out on an evac flight. He phoned me at home and practically ordered me over here to keep watch while you slept.'

Even in her hazy state Allysha could see a gleam of curiosity in Leonie's eyes.

'He knew I was sick when we got back to the airport yesterday,' Allysha explained.

'So he said,' Leonie replied calmly, but the gleam persisted. 'Now, how do you feel? Want a shower? Something to eat?'

Allysha sat up and shook her head experimentally. It hurt when she moved it, but the dreadful throbbing had stopped.

'I think I'm better,' she said cautiously.

'Not quite,' Leonie argued. 'You're sheet-white, and your whole body's trembling with the effort of sitting up. I'll help you across to the bathroom, then put on the kettle. Would you like tea or coffee?'

She moved around the bed as she spoke, and helped Allysha push herself up onto shaky legs. Once upright she felt better.

'I can manage,' she assured Leonie. 'And a cup of tea would be lovely.'

Making her way into the bathroom, she decided that it was just a cold. She tested her throat by swallowing, and found that it wasn't painful or raw. She started the shower and, once under the warm soothing water, she knew the ache in her bones was only stiffness. She'd walked for miles the day before at Wyrangi, climbing the low sand-hills that edged the gulf as she tried to find a good vantage point from which to sketch the hotel—maybe the stiffness was from the exercise.

The thought of her return to sketching made her feel better. She'd learnt drawing from a governess who had been more proficient than talented. Then her first clumsy attempts at oil colours, born out of a need to put the colour she saw around her onto canvas, had frustrated her so much that she'd packed away her pencils and paints and closed her eyes to the splendours she couldn't reproduce.

She lifted her face and let the water run over it. It had taken the simple beauty of the fishing boats at Wyrangi to rekindle the desire to paint. She'd bought a sketching block, pencils, charcoal and crayons. And, tucked away in the bottom of her cupboard, she had new oils.

'Tea's made!'

Turning off the shower, she dried herself hurriedly— clinging to the basin when too sudden a movement left her feeling woozy.

'Thanks, Leonie,' she said when she emerged to find the older woman setting a tray down on the bedside table.

Leonie looked up and smiled, and Allysha thought how attractive she was.

'I'm pleased I was able to help,' Leonie assured her. 'And not only because Nick threatened me with horrible consequences if you were left alone.'

'Nick did that?' The words were little more than a whisper, but Leonie heard them and nodded.

'He was very concerned about you, my dear. More concerned than most colleagues would have been.'

As Allysha picked up her tea-cup she glanced at Leonie, but couldn't see any curiosity in her face. She smiled, knowing that if Susan had made the remark it would have been a demand for information but with Leonie it was a simple statement. A simple statement that made her feel warm and cared for, when she knew it shouldn't!

'Eddie's rostered you off for three days,' Leonie continued. 'You were already due two and he's tacked another one on, but make sure you let him know if you're not better by then. He wouldn't want you taking unnecessary risks with your health.'

'He wouldn't want me taking unnecessary risks with his precious planes, you mean!' Allysha countered, and Leonie grinned and nodded.

'I brought fresh bread, orange juice, some fruit and milk. Do you want any other shopping done?'

Allysha shook her head as gratitude for this simple demonstration of caring threatened to overwhelm her. She *had* shut herself off from human contact for too long!

A noisy banging on her door interrupted her attempts to say thank you and Leonie went to answer it, returning a moment later with a disapproving look on her face.

'There's a group of people outside who say they're friends of yours,' she said. 'Do you want visitors?'

Grimacing at the thought of her 'friends'' impact on Leonie, Allysha sighed and the banging noise continued from the foyer.

'I don't want to see them now—or ever,' she said tiredly. 'They are people I used to know—in another life!'

She paused while she thought the matter through.

'But I should tell them that myself,' she said, mentally preparing for the task ahead. Loud shouts of her name now echoed through the flat.

'Not right now,' Leonie warned, holding up her hand as if to stop her moving. 'I think they're far from sober, and it will only upset you if you try to explain anything to them in their present state.'

'Not sober? What time is it?' She looked down at her watch, then shook her wrist, thinking the numbers it showed must be wrong.

'It's nine o'clock,' Leonie confirmed. 'And I think they're on the way home from last night's fun. They certainly look a little the worse for wear.'

'Well, I can't sit here like a wimp and let you handle them,' Allysha objected. 'You don't know what they're likely to do!'

Leonie touched her arm.

'I'll take care of it,' she repeated. 'I put the chain on the door before I opened it the first time. They won't get in. I'll tell them you're too sick to see them, and if they don't go away I'll call the doorman up from the lobby to remove them. He had no right to let them come up without buzzing you for permission in the first place.'

'He's fairly slack,' Allysha agreed, then she closed her eyes as a particularly loud shout started her head throbbing again.

Leonie disappeared and returned a little later. There were shouts of 'Bye, Allysha,' and 'We'll be back,' from outside, then all was quiet once more.

'You can't stay here and fend off that lot on your own,' Leonie said crisply, and Allysha knew she was right. She wasn't well enough to handle a confrontation with people who lived so frivolously that they would laugh off any protestations that she didn't want to see them.

'Why don't I take you over to Steph's for a few days? She'll be glad to have someone to fuss over. She misses Lucia, you know, and she won't worry you with idle conversation!'

Allysha smiled her relief. It was a brilliant idea but—

'You know I know Aunt Steph?' she asked. She had met Lucia's aunt by accident up at the hospital one day. Allysha had gone up there to visit a patient they had brought in from Caltura. The girl had sat up in the cockpit with her for the flight and talked about how frightened she was, coming to town for the first time. Allysha had assured her that she would visit whenever she could, and one evening Aunt Steph had also been visiting.

'Steph and I have been friends for years,' Leonie said, 'but although I know how generous you've been to Steph's "boarders" I've not told anyone else. Steph told me you wanted the gifts to be anonymous, but how the people who stay with her haven't seen through your little ploy I don't know. The niece who left her clothes with Steph must have had weight fluctuations that took her from size eight to size eighteen!'

Allysha laughed.

'We often wonder if two or three of her guests might come together one day and work out the inconsistencies in the story, but it hasn't happened so far.'

'Well, I think it's doubly good of you,' Leonie told her. 'It's one thing to make donations–people often give because the act of giving makes them feel good— but to give something sensitively so the receiver isn't aware of the gift and doesn't feel the taint of charity—that's special.'

Colouring at the praise, Allysha turned away.

'It's nothing to me,' she muttered uncomfortably, 'but it brings a bit of happiness to them. That's all. It's no big deal!'

She opened her cupboard and pulled out clean underclothes, shirts and shorts. She wouldn't need much for a few days' stay. She was emptying the dirty clothes from her overnight bag when she remembered how she'd come home the previous evening.

'My car's at the airport!' she wailed, upset that her wonderful escape route had been cut off. 'I can't get to Aunt Steph's.'

'And you're sicker than you say you are if you think I'd let you drive across town on your own. I'll take you to Steph's and she'll drop you back or take you to the airport to get your car as soon as you're feeling better.'

Allysha relaxed. It was nice to be fussed over for a change!

Nick put his finger on the doorbell and kept it there, hearing it echo in what he knew was an empty space. It was the fourth time in two days he'd been around to visit Allysha and each time, after he'd rung for more than a reasonable amount of time, he'd actually unlocked the door and gone inside, calling to her as he entered to assure her that he was only there to see if she was OK.

Only she hadn't been there and, try as he might, he couldn't banish the thought that she was with the old crowd who'd been waiting in the lobby when he'd brought her home on Friday afternoon.

He'd rung Leonie three times, knowing she would have been the last person to see Allysha, but she had also disappeared. Foiled there, he'd finally rung Peter, asking—as casually as possible—about Allysha's health.

'She looked so sick on Friday I was worried about her,' he had added weakly.

Peter had sounded startled at first, then puzzled, then concerned about Allysha's health. What he hadn't sounded was lover-like, and when Nick had seen him at the beach on Saturday afternoon with a lissom blonde he'd begun to worry even more about his ex-fiancée.

She hadn't wanted to go to Peter's, he remembered, and the worry turned to a gut-wrenching concern.

'Damn you!' he muttered as he used a spare key he'd taken from her key ring to gain access to her home again. 'Apart from anything else, you're making me feel like a burglar every time I come here, but I can't bear the thought you might have returned and be ill or be upset and need help of some kind.'

But would Allysha ever need his help? he wondered, fighting the urge to linger in her home so that he could feel her presence and absorb her essence from the air.

Of course not! The rebuttal drove him out the door.

And why shouldn't she have gone off for a few days with her friends? Especially if Peter had dropped her for a blonde!

He tried to tell himself that must be the reason, but Peter's presence in Allysha's life was becoming less and less substantial, less and less believable, and somehow that made him feel both better and worse.

'Damn you!' he said again, unfortunately just as the lift doors opened to reveal an affronted-looking matron.

CHAPTER TEN

NICK was sitting in the kitchen at the Base at eight o'clock on Monday morning when Leonie arrived at work.

'I can't find Allysha,' he said baldly, lack of sleep making it impossible to hide his concern.

Leonie frowned at him.

'But I left a message on Jack's machine to say I'd taken her to a friend's place. I'd promised my kids I'd take them up the coast for the weekend, and Allysha wasn't well enough to stay on her own, particularly when there was a crowd of people hanging around that she didn't want to see.'

Nick felt relief swamp through his veins.

'I've a flat of my own,' he said. 'I'm not living at Jack's and our paths didn't cross over the weekend.'

Leonie walked towards him and touched his shoulder.

'I'm sorry,' she said. 'I should have made more of an effort to let you know.'

She paused for a moment, then said, 'She's just up the road, if you'd like to walk up now. You've time before the others get here for the weekly natter.'

But all the doubts he'd ever felt reverberated in his head, and he sat on while 'will I' or 'won't I', 'should I' or 'shouldn't I', plagued him with their insistent echoes.

He glanced at his watch, and used an old excuse to buy some time.

170

'She might be sleeping now; I'll go when I finish work,' he told Leonie.

'I would if I were you,' she said quietly, then she walked away, leaving him with all the unanswered questions.

'Phone for you, Allysha,' Aunt Steph called from the kitchen where she was preparing the evening meal. Allysha stood up from the comfortable squatter's chair on the wide veranda and walked reluctantly inside. 'It's Eddie Stone,' Aunt Steph added, passing the receiver to her visitor.

'How are you?' Eddie asked, and Allysha knew that it wasn't an idle question.

'One hundred per cent,' she told him.

'Sure?' he persisted, then he listened while she reassured him.

'What's up?' she asked.

'It's an evac out at Talgoola. Semi with a load of sheep off the road. The fellow's in a bad way and Jack wants him out immediately, but I've run out of operational hours for today.'

'You've got four other pilots,' Allysha reminded him, but excitement was stirring. What she needed was a challenge to pull her out of the despondency the cold had left as its aftermath.

'It'll be a road landing,' Eddie said gloomily. 'Michael did a day clinic flight today so he's out, and Bill's at Wooli. If you're well I know you can handle it. The local copper has people pulling out the roadside posts, but there's a bridge.'

Of course there was, Allysha thought. The railings on bridges were much harder to remove than roadside guideposts.

'How wide and how high?' she asked. The wing-tips on both models of the King Airs they used had a good clearance above the ground, but if the bridge was narrow the underslung engines, tucked in close to the body of the plane, would hit the railings.

'It's two lanes and the road takes a lot of heavy traffic, so they'd be wide lanes. You'd have plenty of space for the engines to get through, and your wings will clear the railings.'

It sounded simple enough, but Allysha knew that the reality was otherwise. Thundering down the road towards the bridge, it would appear as narrow as a country lane and the railings would loom closer and higher in her eyes.

'I can do it,' she told Eddie. 'I'll get out to the airport now and check the maps. Who's coming with me?'

'Jack and Susan,' Eddie told her.

'Two people? It must be serious!'

'The fellow had his family with him,' Eddie said quietly, and Allysha guessed that someone had been killed.

'I'll drive you to the airport,' Aunt Steph said. She had been hovering by the phone and had heard enough to know that her guest had been called out.

Jack and Susan were waiting by the phone. Jeff had wheeled out the bigger C200 rather than the smaller C90. Allysha would have preferred the smaller plane, but the medical crew must have decided that they would need the more sophisticated equipment on the emergency aircraft.

'How are you with roads and bridges?' Jack said as they took off.

'Apparently better than anyone else Eddie had on

call,' Allysha told him, banking smoothly to head towards the western plains.

The controls felt sweet beneath her fingers and the thrill of flying, which never seemed to diminish, filtered its happiness into her bloodstream.

Lanterns of some kind, at first no brighter than a glow-worm's light, lined the part of the road marked out for landing. Allysha said a silent prayer. Many roads around the country had been especially strengthened to make emergency landing strips, but this stretch had been chosen simply because it was close to the scene of the accident and ran straight for enough distance for a plane to land and take off without having to turn.

She circled once to get her bearings and then slowly brought the plane down and circled again, noticing the bridge halfway along the illuminated strip of bitumen.

'Here goes, gang,' she said tightly. They dropped onto the road, bounced and settled. The bridge rushed towards her, closing in on itself exactly as she'd known it would.

The big thing is not to panic, she reminded herself. If you panic and unbalance the plane you're in trouble.

'A policeman measured it,' she said, reassuring herself as much as Jack, but she heard him suck in his breath and knew that he was leaning towards her, willing the plane to shrink in on itself.

'We're through it,' she told him, holding the shuddering power lever as it fought the forward thrust of the plane's momentum.

'And how do you take off again?' Jack asked, peering into the darkness which was made more absolute by hammering rain. 'You can't turn here—it's too wet once you're off the bitumen. You'd be bogged for sure.'

'I take off in the same direction,' she told him,

repeating the instructions she'd received from Eddie in mid-flight. 'There are no more bridges, only a hotel we might hit, going that way!'

Jack grinned at her, then said, 'Are you coming with us?'

She braked to a halt.

'Do you think you'll need me?'

He nodded.

'There were two adults and three kids in the semi-trailer, Allysha. The woman's been killed and the man is fighting for his life. I'd like someone to hold onto the kids for me, if that's OK with you.'

It was her turn to nod, not wanting Jack to hear the tightness in her voice.

She followed him into the cabin. Susan was handing equipment out through the open door to someone who was only a voice.

'That's a Thomas pack, a stretcher, the monitor, extra respiration units for the kids, splints and neck braces, drugs.' She listed the equipment for Jack.

'Good girl! Now grab a coat and let's go!' he said and, shrugging into a waterproof coat, he led the way out into the rain.

The voice had belonged to the policeman, Allysha realised as they piled into the big Land Cruiser for the journey up the road to the accident site.

They heard the painful bleating of injured sheep before they reached the wreckage.

'I'll start shooting them as soon as you've got your patients away,' the policeman said. 'The publican offered to start, but somehow I couldn't do it while the kids were there.'

Allysha felt her stomach tighten with anguish, but she knew that he was right. Injured stock had to be put down as humanely as possible, and few of the sheep in the two-storeyed trailer would have escaped unscathed.

The police vehicle pulled up beside a tarpaulin erected over the cabin of the huge prime mover, and Jack and Susan leapt out. Allysha followed more slowly, crossing to the man who seemed to be in charge at the scene.

'Where are the children?' she asked. 'I'll keep an eye on them if you like.'

'They were asleep in the cabin behind the driver—strapped in, thank heavens, and uninjured. My wife took them back to the pub,' the man told her. 'She's going to contact the grandparents. They live a bit further out of town but they'll come in and take care of them.'

'Are they nice people?' Allysha asked, although she knew that it was a stupid question. What was the man likely to say?

'Very nice,' he assured her.

Had someone said that about her grandmother? she wondered as she made her way back towards the temporary shelter where Jack and Susan were working to stabilise their patient. As she drew closer she found herself praying that they would save the man—that the children would have one parent to give them the love and understanding they would need.

'His breathing's very shallow and he seems to be gasping—should I switch to positive pressure oxygen to help him?' Susan asked. Jack was inside the cab itself, and Allysha guessed that their patient would be wedged against the steering-wheel. Airways first, she reminded herself. Airways, breathing, circulation!

'No way,' Jack replied. 'If he has a tension pneumo-thorax with air leaking from his lungs to his chest positive pressure will exacerbate it. Shine the light over this way and let's have another look at him.'

Allysha saw the torchlight move, and knew that the conditions were fighting against them.

'He's cyanotic; it's hard to tell from where he is if his trachea is deviated but I'd guess at it, and there's definitely hyperresonance on percussion,' Jack said. 'It's got to be a tension pneumothorax. I'm going to put a needle in and use a flutter valve to regulate the inhalations, then he should be right on oxygen until we get him out.'

Susan murmured something and bent over the bulky pack which was spread open on the ground.

The policeman arrived with a pressure lantern, and moved beneath the tarpaulin to give them more illumination.

'Allysha, there's a green immobilising device in that small bag—looks like a corset—could you get it out?'

She bent down to retrieve the smaller bag, and pulled at the Velcro straps that held it closed.

The green padded vest did indeed look like a corset, but she had seen them before and knew that it could be wrapped around the torso of an accident victim and secured. Handles on the side made it easy for rescuers to pull the victim free. The device stabilised the spine, but left openings for Jack's flutter valve or other medical paraphernalia to obtrude.

She walked across and passed it up to Jack, then Susan called for fluid and she crossed to the Thomas pack and found the bag Susan wanted and a sealed pack of infusion equipment—needle catheter, tubing, and taps.

Passing these to Susan, she noticed that Jack had fitted a cervical collar and the green vest to his patient. She stepped back out of the way, waiting for instructions before she helped retrieve him from the cabin. As she moved aside for the policeman to get closer, she noticed the shrouded figure lying at the far edge of the shelter provided by the tarpaulin.

Her heart clenched and she thought, as she rarely did, of the stories she'd gleaned about her parents' accidental deaths. It had been a lonely road like this one, but no one had found them until it was too late.

'I'll put the lamp down here and give those two a hand to get him out,' the policeman said. 'The doc wants to get the fella straight to hospital. Says he's bleeding badly internally.'

Allysha moved aside, then noticed that the shrouded figure wasn't quite protected by the tarp and water was falling directly onto the concealing blanket. She walked across, not sure what she could do but knowing that she had to do something, then heard a cry and turned.

A sheet of flame blotted out the scene, then pain so fierce she couldn't scream burned in her eyes and she was flying through the air, caught in wet tarpaulin that wrapped itself around her like a shroud.

'I'll take her,' a deep voice said, and she knew that it was Nick and tried to find him in the darkness.

'Let the ambulance men handle it, Nick!'

Peter's voice? Why were there two doctors on the flight? And how did she know she'd been on a flight—because she did know!

'The ambulance will take her straight to hospital,' Peter added. 'Jack phoned ahead—there's an ophthalmologist standing by.'

'Do you love her?' Nick again, but love whom?

'We were and are friends, Nick, nothing more.'

Was it good that Peter and Nick were friends? she

wondered muzzily. Or didn't it matter? She tried to
think but the darkness made her brain feel foggy.

'And, as a friend, I'll go with her to the hospital.'

'No! I'll go with her.' That was Nick—a simple but
definite statement of intention. If it hadn't been so dark
she would have smiled at him because he was showing
his stubborn streak, and she'd often teased him about it.

But Nick wasn't hers to tease any more, she
remembered, and sadness bit into her mind.

Then someone was holding her hand and, as the
fingers rubbed along hers, she knew it was Nick—
knew his skin, his touch and the feel of his long, slender
fingers entwining in hers.

'Where are you, Nick?' she asked. 'Why can't I
see you?'

But she didn't hear the words come out and when
she tried again she felt the fingers touch her shoulder,
and slide along her neck, and heard him say, 'You'll
be all right, my darling. I'm here with you; you know
that, don't you?'

His voice sounded hoarse and she wanted to ask if
he had a cold, but her mouth wasn't working properly.
The movement that had told her they were in a vehicle
stopped, and there was a rattling noise, then she was
being moved again, although the sensation was peculiar
in the dense blackness of her new world.

'Is she conscious?' someone asked, and she tried to
tell them that she was, then remembered that her mouth
wouldn't work.

'This is Jack, Allysha. I'm taking hold of your hand.
I'm going to ask you questions and want you to squeeze
my fingers—once for yes, and twice for no.'

She heard the words and wondered why Jack was
speaking to her in such a slow, strange manner.

'Do you understand?'

Of course I do, she wanted to tell him, but I want Nick to hold my hand, not you.

'I'll talk to her, Jack,' she heard Nick say quietly, and felt his fingers reclaim her hand.

Squeeze once for yes, Jack had said. She squeezed and felt Nick's fingers tighten convulsively on hers.

'Allysha, there was an explosion at the accident site,' he said. 'You were thrown out of the way, but it seems you must have turned as the petrol tank went up and your eyes and face are burnt.'

No! No! No! She squeezed and kept on squeezing, a denial that was shouting in her mind but unable to be spoken.

'Your lungs may have been damaged by the heat, so Jack has a tube in place to help you breathe. We are at the hospital now. Your burns will be dressed and a specialist will look at your eyes. I'll be here all the time, darling, so don't be worried.'

He'd called her darling before, she remembered. Maybe she hadn't lost Nick after all; maybe his going away was a dream, like the blackness.

Words flew around in the dark—words like radiation injury, possible ocular ischaemia, some corneal scarring to be expected, perhaps corneal transplants later, hard to tell.

The words weren't all said at once and often she fancied that she was sleeping in between hearing them, but the blackness remained constant.

'Allysha!'

'Nick?'

She heard the word come out and was amazed.

'My voice is working again,' she said, forcing the words from a sore, raspy throat.

'The doctor removed the endotracheal tube,' Nick told her, his fingers stroking at the skin of her hand. 'How are you feeling?'

'My throat hurts,' she told him, 'and I think my head aches, but it's so dark, Nick, it's hard to think. Why's it dark?'

His fingers moved up her arm, gentle on her skin, touching reassuringly.

Reassuringly? Why reassuringly?

'What's wrong?' she asked, feeling panic rise like a thick fog in her chest. 'Tell me what's wrong, Nick!'

'Your eyes were burnt,' he said quietly, the soothing fingers trailing on her skin. 'An explosion is sometimes too fast for the blink reflex to protect the eyes. At the moment your eyelids are swollen because they were also burnt. You wouldn't be able to open your eyes anyway, so they're taped shut.'

'And behind the swollen eyelids?' she asked.

'We'll know in a few days,' he told her. 'It may be that you escaped with superficial damage.'

'And if I didn't?' she said as panic percolated through her body. Not blind! she wanted to cry. I can't be blind!

'If you didn't, if there is more damage, there are options later on, Allysha.'

'What options? What could be wrong? I don't want to know later on; I want to know now.'

She tried to control the terror she felt but part of her knew that she must sound like the spoilt brat she'd once been. Nick hadn't liked that Allysha, and she wanted so badly for him to like her now.

'There's a chance you might develop heat cataracts, but they can be removed by surgery. If there's been corneal scarring you could lose some sight, but remember that a corneal implant could restore it.'

The enormity of what he was saying sank in.

'I couldn't fly,' she whispered as the repercussions of her injury finally struck her. 'And I'd never see the sunset again.'

She wanted to cry but didn't know if blind eyes would shed tears, and, anyway, she *never* cried.

'There are other things you can do beside flying,' Nick whispered huskily, and she wondered if he was crying for her. 'You can marry me, for one. I'll tell you about the sunsets, Lys; I'll describe every one of them for you so in your mind you see them in all their splendid colours.'

Sadness and despair crept through her.

'Why, Nick?' she asked. 'Why marriage? Why now? Because I'm going to be helpless and dependent? Will that make us more equal in some way?'

She turned away from where he must be sitting, unable to bear the agony of her thoughts.

'Go away, Nick,' she added quietly. 'Go away and don't ever come back.'

He didn't go away. He didn't talk to her, or argue, but nor did he go! She felt his presence in a tingling up her spine, then as a warmth—like an extra blanket—and eventually she slept.

'Nick's out on a flight but he'll be back later.'

Leonie's voice.

'I don't want him to come back,' Allysha said.

'Maybe not,' was the reply, 'but I think he'll come anyway.'

She refused to speak to him, although at times she felt so furious that she wanted to yell at his stubborn persistence. Slowly she worked out which bits of her were bandaged. One hand and arm, and it seemed—

by feeling with her good hand—that all her face was covered.

'I'm going to unwrap your eyes.' The doctor's voice—and with it fear so great that it filled her mind.

'I'm here with you, Lys.' Nick's voice! Nick's fingers holding hers! She wanted to tell him to go away, but she wasn't talking to him so she clung to the fingers and stayed silent.

She felt hands moving against her head, then the doctor said, 'The room is dark, Allysha, because your eyes will be sensitive to light. I want you to try to open your eyes, but don't panic if you can't see clearly straight away.'

Nick's fingers tightened on hers, reassuring and encouraging.

She tried to open her eyelids, and flinched at the pain. Was the darkness less intense? She didn't know. Silly tears welled up, then Nick said, 'Look at me, Allysha!' and she turned towards his voice and saw a shadow move.

'Your eyelids are still very swollen,' the doctor told her, 'which is why it hurts to open them and why your field of vision is severely limited.'

A light shone in the darkness, and her fingers tightened convulsively on Nick's.

'I saw a light,' she whispered, then she repeated it, louder and stronger. 'I saw a light!'

'That's great,' the doctor said. 'Now, I'll tell you what happens next.'

She didn't listen properly to what happened next because Nick's lips were pressing on her fingers, his teeth rubbing against her knuckles, and his breathing, cool on her damp skin, seemed ragged and uneven.

'. . .dark glasses. . .no risks. . .mask. . .other specialist.'

Hand on her head again, sliding something over her ears. She lifted her heavy lids again and saw the shadows darker than before. Nick squeezed her fingers one more time and then he put her hand on the edge of the bed.

'I've got to go to work,' he whispered, and she heard him walk away.

Leonie came again, and it was she who filled in all the details of the accident.

'So Jack and Susan had lifted the patient away from the truck before the petrol tank exploded?' Allysha asked when Leonie finished talking.

'Yes, with the help of the policeman. Because of the way the cabin had slewed off the road, they were protected by the trailer full of sheep,' she confirmed. 'You were the closest and probably would have been thrown clear and escaped any injury if the policeman hadn't realised what was about to happen and call out to you.'

'I remember turning around. What happened next?'

'Eddie flew another plane out with Greg Roberts on board. He landed on the road behind your plane, which was already loaded with the injured man and yourself, and Greg flew the C200 back with Eddie following.'

Having assimilated this, Allysha lay still for a moment in the darkened room, her eyes hidden behind the dark glasses she had to wear. Then she asked the final question—the one she hadn't wanted to ask any-one earlier.

'I can't see what I look like, Leonie, because my eyes won't open, but I'm not stupid. If my eyes were burnt, then my face must be. Is it bad? Is that why no one will talk about it?'

'Oh, Allysha, you should have said something earlier.'

Allysha felt soft fingers on her cheek.

'Your face is as lovely as ever. There were superficial burns, of course, and you've no eyebrows to speak of, but the doctors think you must have had your hands up to your face because the back of one hand and arm is burnt. . .'

The woman! She'd been walking across to the woman and wiping tears away from her eyes!

'Did the man survive? The children's father?'

It seemed impossible that she didn't know!

'He'll be in hospital for a while, but he will survive.'

Not Leonie's voice at all!

'Oh, Nick, to think I hadn't given him a thought. I've been lying here feeling sorry for myself, not knowing if he was alive or dead or if the children still had a parent.'

Her fingers scrabbled on the sheet until she felt his hand. She grasped it tightly, and hoped he'd forgotten that she'd told him to go away.

'Those kids will have a better deal than you, Lys,' he whispered, and she felt his lips brush against her cheek.

'Leonie said my lips aren't burnt,' she said, opening her eyes as far as they would go and straining to see his face to guess at his reaction!

'You told me to go away,' he reminded her. 'I could hardly kiss you when I was pretending I wasn't here.'

'I hoped you might have forgotten that,' she told him. 'I didn't want your pity, Nick, your charity.'

'But did you want my love?' he asked, his voice so husky it seemed to rasp against her skin.

'You didn't mention love—you mentioned marriage!'

'But you should have understood the love,' he said, and now his lips touched hers. 'Damn it, Lys, I loved the early version to distraction in spite of all your efforts to turn my life into utter chaos. Back then I was terrified I would lose you; that you'd grow bored with me and go off to play with someone else. That stupid, tortuous fear overshadowed everything until, in the end, it won and I walked away from you. But now. . .'

'But now?' she murmured, her heartbeats hammering in her eyes.

'And now I see what you've achieved I look at the person you've become and terrified is too weak a word for what I feel. Why would you want to have anything to do with me? I ask myself. How could you fall in love with someone who hurt you so badly once before? Someone who could never be worthy of your love?'

'It must be fate,' she whispered, and lifted her hand to touch his face. 'I can see your nose,' she said, running one finger along it. 'And your eyebrows, and your lips! But they're too far away to kiss.'

He leant towards her and she felt his mouth fasten on to hers, and a shudder of delight ran through her body. His hands slid behind her back and, very gently, he lifted her and held her close against his warmth.

The kiss deepened and memories she'd thought were locked away for ever slid through her nerves, firing her body with an aching hunger.

'Can we lock the door?' she whispered, and felt his shocked withdrawal.

'I'd forgotten where we were,' he muttered, still holding her tightly and pressing little kisses to her ear, her neck, the corner of her mouth!

Allysha relaxed in his arms, giving herself up to sensations she hadn't felt for twelve months, delighting in the touch and feel of this man she loved so much.

Then suddenly it stopped, and she was lying back against the pillows once more.

'What did you say?' Nick demanded and she looked towards his voice.

'About loving you? About marriage?' She smiled at his impatience. 'I don't think I said anything!'

'Not about that,' he said impatiently, brushing aside such minor considerations. 'About seeing my nose, my eyebrows.'

She reached up and touched his nose and then ran her finger along his eyebrows, and he grasped her shoulders and shook her gently.

'You can see them? You can see?'

She blinked, surprised by his amazement.

'They're a bit hazy, and dark because of the glasses,' she explained, 'but yes, I can see them. You kept telling me I would, but that it would take time.'

'Oh, my darling!' he sighed, and held her close again. 'I kept telling you that and praying I was right, because it wasn't ever that certain.'

She ran her fingers through his hair, which still needed cutting by the feel of it.

'It's not certain, Nick,' she reminded him. 'I know there could be some loss of sight or complications later, but someone said he'd tell me about the sunsets. If he keeps that promise I'll be able to cope with everything else.'

She felt his arms tighten, and drew strength from the silent vow.

'Kissing the patients, Doctor?' a light voice said, and they sprang apart.

'Hello, Katie,' Nick said, to let Allysha know who was visiting. 'Come in and talk to my fiancée.'

MILLS & BOON®

Medical Romance™

COMING NEXT MONTH

A MIDWIFE'S CHALLENGE by Frances Crowne

Katy Woods resolved never to get involved with men after her disastrous marriage to a bigamist—until she met Dr Mark Hammond. He was irresistible—until she discovered the truth about his ex-girlfriend, which was a haunting reminder of her past...

FULL RECOVERY by Lilian Darcy

Camberton Hospital

Helen Darnell suspected her husband of twenty years, Nick, to be having an affair with a beautiful doctor. Helen tried to quell her fears believing that Nick was faithful to her. Their marriage was teetering on the edge of destruction and only one thing could save it—the truth.

DOCTOR ACROSS THE LAGOON by Margaret Holt

Lucinda Hallcross-Spriggs' journey to Italy for a medical conference took an unexpected turn when she met the devilishly handsome Dr Pino Ponti. She soon succumbed to his relentless charm, but with his restless heart and uneasy past, she surely had no part to play in his future.

LAKELAND NURSE by Gill Sanderson

Zanne Ripley's application for Medical School was unsuccessful—and all because of Dr Neil Calder. Now she had to work with him at the Mountain Activities Centre, but his charm soon broke down her defences. But Neil had a secret...

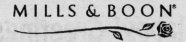

'Happy' Greetings!

Would you like to win a year's supply of Mills & Boon® books? Well you can and they're free! Simply complete the competition below and send it to us by 31st August 1997. The first five correct entries picked after the closing date will each win a year's subscription to the Mills & Boon series of their choice. What could be easier?

ACSPPMTHYHARSI

_____ _____

TPHEEYPSARA

_____ _____

RAHIHPYBDYTAP

_____ _____

NHMYRTSPAAPNEREUY

_____ ___ ____

DYVLTEPYAANINSEPAH

_____ _____ ___

YAYPNAHPEREW

_____ ___ ____

DMHPYAHRYOSETPA

_____ _____ ___

VRHPYNARSAEYNPIA

_____ _____

Please turn over for details of how to enter ☞

How to enter...

There are eight jumbled up greetings overleaf, most of which you will probably hear at some point throughout the year. Each of the greetings is a 'happy' one, i.e. the word 'happy' is somewhere within it. All you have to do is identify each greeting and write your answers in the spaces provided. Good luck!

When you have unravelled each greeting don't forget to fill in your name and address in the space provided and tick the Mills & Boon® series you would like to receive if you are a winner. Then simply pop this page into an envelope (you don't even need a stamp) and post it today. Hurry—competition ends 31st August 1997.

Mills & Boon 'Happy' Greetings Competition
FREEPOST, Croydon, Surrey, CR9 3WZ

Please tick the series you would like to receive if you are a winner

Presents™ ❏   Enchanted™ ❏   Medical Romance™ ❏
Historical Romance™ ❏   Temptation® ❏

Are you a Reader Service Subscriber?   Yes ❏   No ❏

Ms/Mrs/Miss/Mr _____
(BLOCK CAPS PLEASE)

Address _____

_____

_____ Postcode _____

(I am over 18 years of age)

C7B